Millie's Honor

MILLIE'S HONOR

A Novel

Neal Powers

iUniverse, Inc.
New York Lincoln Shanghai

Millie's Honor

Copyright © 2008 by Neal L. Powers

All rights reserved. No part of this book may be used or reproduced by any means, graphic, electronic, or mechanical, including photocopying, recording, taping or by any information storage retrieval system without the written permission of the publisher except in the case of brief quotations embodied in critical articles and reviews.

iUniverse books may be ordered through booksellers or by contacting:

iUniverse
2021 Pine Lake Road, Suite 100
Lincoln, NE 68512
www.iuniverse.com
1-800-Authors (1-800-288-4677)

Because of the dynamic nature of the Internet, any Web addresses or links contained in this book may have changed since publication and may no longer be valid.

This is a work of fiction. All of the characters, names, incidents, organizations, and dialogue in this novel are either the products of the author's imagination or are used fictitiously.

ISBN: 978-0-595-47224-6 (pbk)
ISBN: 978-0-595-91507-1 (ebk)

Printed in the United States of America

To Mary Stahr, whose love and support helped bring Millie to life.

Acknowledgments

I owe a special debt of gratitude to The Reverend Holly Davis and to her exceptional husband, Van Davis. It is she who encouraged me to write this novel, and he who provided valuable insights and suggestions to improve the story. Thank you both for your friendship, encouragement, and for honoring me by being my first readers.

I am also deeply indebted to Ted Shank, whose candid accounts of his Vietnam experience inspired Raymond's story. Ted's battlefield promotion, Purple Hearts, and medals for valor, both a Bronze and a Silver Star, are real. My characters are not. If I got any part of his story right, it is to his credit. The parts I got wrong are the product of my own imagination.

I must also thank the staff at iUniverse for their skillful assistance. I appeared on their doorstep with a big idea and a satchel full of bits and pieces. They helped me find my way. Finally, to the long-suffering English teachers who taught me to love books, this is my way of saying thank you. I am sorry to turn it in so late.

Prologue

▼

The Barn

October 1959

Like eyes peering through a thousand tiny holes, the setting sun riddles the darkness inside. It is the time of day that proves that barns are part of the great outdoors, even those covered with wood and corrugated tin. Light spills into the hayloft, splashing across a humming hemp rope with one end tied to a diagonal brace, the other end disappearing over a distant rafter.

Soon, the thrashing at the far end of the rope ceases, and the barn falls silent except for the creak of rope against wood—the sound of a pendulum under an unbearable load. At the other end of the rope hangs the body of seventy-eight-pound Donny Weber, age thirteen, naked as the day he was born.

The secrets of his life drain away, the aroma of his waste mingling with that of livestock long since slaughtered. Soon enough will come the calling, the screaming, the cursing, the fistfights, and the lying—endless lying. But for now, in the autumn of 1959, at the end of a life far too brief to bear fruit, there is only silence—and the creaking of a rope.

Chapter 1

Raleigh

Half a million years ago, give or take a hundred thousand years, an icy mass the size of Antarctica ground past Chicago on its way south. At its southernmost reach, its gleaming face carved a line on the earth we now call the Missouri River. Spanning all the way to New York, the eastern shoulder of the Laurentide Ice Sheet also gouged out the Ohio River Valley. Desperate for a path to the ocean, the Ohio and Missouri Rivers joined forces to cut the Mississippi River. It wasn't trickle-down; it was cataclysmic. What sometimes begins as innocently as a snowflake can become a force to change the landscape. It is not unlike the affairs of men.

Few in Raleigh care that the hill on which the courthouse stands is the spot where the great white giant paused for thousands of years before melting its way back north. They are too busy farming. In the summers, the flat land north of town stands tall with corn and soybeans. The city sprang up where the good soil played out.

To the south and below the courthouse, creeks and streams tumble downhill in search of the wide, flat bottomland of the great river. To be a Raleigh County crop farmer means working either the river bottoms between floods or the northern croplands between droughts. Livestock farmers on the hilly land in between survive as long as the wells and feed hold out.

Towns like Raleigh do not have time for operas. There is too much work to do. That accounts for its slave trade in the early 1800s, the blood spilled during the Civil War, and the smoldering bigotry which lingered through the 1950s. Into this heritage comes a new generation, one whose definition of normal is rooted in what Raleigh used to be, not in what it could become.

Car Spotting

June 1957

"Ford," said Raymond. It was his turn.

"You're kidding me. You see a machine like that, and all you can say is Ford? Next, you'll tell us it's blue." Wally ran the game because he knew the most cars.

"All right, hotshot," Raymond said, tracking the passing car. "It's a 1950 Ford Custom Deluxe, and it's blue. And it has 47,000 miles on the odometer."

"How did you know all that?"

"Superior skill and knowledge, my good man. Of course, it helps that it was Grandpa."

"Yeah, well, you didn't recognize him until he was right on top of us."

Bud griped about the spotting distance whenever Raymond was right. It didn't matter. It was still a point for Raymond. He grinned. Bud had so much to learn.

Between passing cars, the boys sprawled under a lilac bush. Its heavy foliage provided shade from the searing heat of the sun. They could watch for northbound cars and play with the sweet smelling petals that showered down on them. The scent also attracted honeybees, so occasionally the boys had to scamper out of the way. Even though the summer was young, their arms and faces were already the color of honey.

A quarter of a mile away, the cars disappeared into the valley. Exactly twenty-three seconds later, they should reappear, rising over the hill toward them. Speeders popped up early. The boys knew who they were.

The trick was to be on the top rung of the fence, without appearing to hurry, by the time the car went by. If they mounted the fence too late, it cost a penalty point. If they scrambled too soon, it cost two.

"Here comes another one," Raymond said, nudging Wally. "It's your turn."

"Well, my merry men," Wally said, mounting the fence with deliberate nonchalance, "the bullet-shaped nose makes me believe it's a Studebaker." Wally was the tallest of them and was slump-shouldered and awkward in his movements. The car disappeared into the valley.

"Yeah, well, we could all see it was green," Bud said. He seemed to be stuck on colors.

None of them realized he needed glasses. Months from now, Mrs. Blackwell would make an offhand remark in the presence of the school nurse about his poor reading. Nurse Maysie would figure it out. Most of the kids in Raleigh who wore glasses had her to thank for it.

Over the hill came a 1951 Studebaker Champion. Wally pulled off an imaginary hat and took a bow as it whizzed by. Raymond spotted a '49 Buick Roadmaster but mistook a '52 Oldsmobile for a Chrysler Imperial. By the time the sun started going down, the score was 6 to 5 to 3 in favor of Wally. That was when it happened. As Raymond would say years later, "It was the damnedest thing any of us ever saw. Of course, we were only twelve."

A Model T came over the hill. They gawked as it approached making a distinctive pockity-pockity-pockity sound. When the driver leaned out the widow to wave, red hair flashed in the sunlight. It was the first glimpse any of them ever had of Miss Millie, but it burned into their memories forever. She was gorgeous. And she was driving the most unusual car in the world.

Raymond, wiry and quick, bolted for his bike. He pushed it up out of the ditch and peeled out after her. Wally was right behind him, bike wagging from side to side as he pumped for all he was worth. The big boys tore off, leaving little Bud standing in the ditch.

"Hey, wait a minute! Where are you guys going?"

Raymond raced through traffic to see where she might be heading. Some folks went to the bank or the post office, but others parked on Main Street to run errands. The Model T waited at Raleigh's only traffic light. When it turned green, the car continued north.

Bud finally found his pals in front of the high school. The Model T stood by the curb. After a brief huddle, they decided to hang out at the gas station on the corner. Before long, all three bikes were upside down on the handlebars, wheels spinning. Never had six bike tires received so much attention.

Gilroy Ferguson, the attendant, kept a wary eye on the boys. They teased him too much, calling him "Goofy Gil the Gas Guy," and were always riding back and forth across the rubber hose, bouncing their bikes to ring the bell, yelling stuff like, "Fill 'er up, Gil, and don't forget the windshield this time." Now, the same boys were hanging out at the air hose. They had to be up to something. It made him uneasy.

Raymond recognized the tractor-like sound before he turned to see it. There she was, pulling into the station and up to the pump. She asked Goofy Gil for a fill-up. He was flummoxed. Mashing his Phillips 66 hat to his heart, he started bowing, like she was royalty or something. She smiled. He blushed and completely forgot where he was.

She leaned out the window, aimed her thumb toward the gas tank, and said, "Gas, remember?" Gil came to his senses and stumbled for the pump. Her laughter hung in the air like music.

Unable to stand it anymore, Wally went around to the driver's door. "Hey, Lady, I ain't ever seen such a sight. What in the hell kind of car is it?"

"How old are you, young man?"

"Thirteen, well, I mean, I will be in October. Why?"

"Because by the time you get to my English class, I hope you will have learned how to address a lady. Swearing is not the best way to make a favorable impression." It was the first time Raymond or Bud ever saw their leader stupefied, unable to find words.

"Since you asked, it's a 1925 Model T Ford. Dad got it when he started his practice, and he was right. He said if I wanted to be noticed today, I should drive the Model T."

Raymond spilled his guts. "Lady, you coulda rode in on top of a load o' watermelon and still got yourself noticed."

"Well, hello there, sailor!" She smiled at Raymond. "I believe you mean 'I could have ridden in on top of a load of watermelons and still been noticed.' But thanks for the compliment."

Raymond blushed and looked away. She paid Goofy Gil and drove off laughing, leaving them standing in silence on the oil-stained ramp, the aroma of asphalt, antifreeze, and gasoline swirling around them. Like perplexed Indians studying Pilgrims rowing ashore, their notion of home was about to change.

No one saw the Model T again, but it served its purpose. To this day, some swear she never owned a car. Others claim she drove a Nash. That's the problem with legends. The lines get blurred between the way we want to remember things, and the way they really were. Millie did not own a car until she paid cash for a '62 Buick Special. She got it because it was *Motor Trend's* Car of the Year. On a whim, she got the V8 instead of the V6 and discovered she could make hot-rodders mind their manners.

Meanwhile, the sweaty summer of 1957 melted into August like a pocketful of chocolate. God had ordained it for swimming, playing softball, and snatching feelers out of flooded holes. For Raymond, hunting crawdads with a garden hose was the perfect sport. He did not know it was his last innocent summer.

Chapter 2

The Courthouse

Last Week of August 1957

Wally, Raymond, and Bud rode in tight circles in the middle of the street. The high-speed run down Mallinckrodt Hill had been exhilarating; their unbuttoned shirts flapping behind them like capes. Speed provided temporary relief from the hundred-degree heat.

"So what do you want to do now?" asked Wally.

"We could go up to Barclay's and watch TV in the window," suggested Bud.

"It's too early for that," Raymond said, dodging toward the curb to keep from running over Bud. "Cartoons haven't started yet. Nothing on now but soap operas."

"Ugh," said Bud. "The guy who invented television must want to puke."

"Well, how about the park? There's plenty of stuff to do there," said Wally.

"Cool." And they were off like a line of hornets.

That was when they discovered Miss Millie had moved to town. At the end of the block near the park entrance, Raymond noticed a pink and purple Schwinn behind a forsythia bush. He didn't give it much thought. It was a girl's bike. But there on the porch steps, scratching a mongrel behind the ears, sat Miss Millie. The "Room for Rent" sign was missing from Mama Rosa's picket fence. She taught piano lessons to half the kids in town and made the best chocolate chip cookies ever.

"Good morning, ma'am," they called as they rode past.

She waved and shaded her eyes, answering, "Don't be so formal. Miss Millie will do."

Later, waiting for a snapping turtle to surface in the pond, Bud said what was on his mind. "I don't get it. We call all our teachers 'ma'am.' I thought we were being polite."

"We were," Raymond said thoughtfully. "But I'm beginning to think she ain't gonna be no ordinary teacher. What say you, Sir Robin of Locksley?"

Wally thought for a moment before he answered. "It looks to me like she ain't never been ordinary, and she ain't never gonna be." They pondered that in silence.

Bud whacked Raymond on the arm and said, "Well, hello there, sailor! Did you see who rode into town on that load of watermelons?"

Raymond grabbed Bud in a headlock, rolling him back and forth on the ground, alternately giggling and growling. Then he let go and flopped onto his stomach. His pals sprawled out beside him as he studied a long stem of grass, plucked it, and began to chew.

"Guess what?" he said.

"What?"

"I think we're going to have to learn to talk good English."

"Nunh unh."

"Are too."

"Ain't never."

"Are too."

"No way."

"Wanna bet?"

"Naw, you're probably right."

"Damn."

"You can say that again."

Days later, they spotted Miss Millie pedaling to town. In seconds, she had escorts.

"Hello, Miss Millie. Where are you going?" Wally asked as he pulled alongside.

"Hi, boys. I'm going to get groceries."

"Which store?"

"Is there a choice?"

"Oh sure, there's the Piggly Wiggly, a Kroger's up north, and Miller's Meat Market on the corner by the post office. It stinks. Old Man Miller says it's aging beef, but I say it's rotten meat. The thing is that he makes deliveries. He hauls boxes of groceries right to your house and leaves them on the back porch. He'll even put them inside if you want. At least that way, you don't have to smell the store. But I still smell it on the boxes. Anyway, there are corner grocers all over town, but mostly Mama sends me to the Piggly Wiggly."

"Then that's where I'll go. How about showing me the way?"

The boys pulled ahead and spread out single file. They took the shortest route, cutting through several alleys she would not have chosen.

"It's okay," Bud yelled back over his shoulder. "Ride fast and the old ladies won't have time to scold you." Millie picked up the pace.

There was something different about her. She talked to them like adults. She listened when no one else did. Their teachers were usually friendly until the end of school. She was more like a friend who couldn't help that she was a teacher. Over the next few days, the boys showed her their favorite shortcuts, except for the ones through people's yards. Those were reserved for getaways. Grown-ups didn't need them—or so they thought.

School began on the third day of September, under a cloud of national disgrace. In Little Rock, Arkansas, Governor Orval Faubus called out the National Guard to prevent a handful of black children from attending Central High School. Suddenly, racial bigotry was televised into living rooms all across America—in black and white. President Eisenhower stripped Faubus of his troops by "federalizing" the Arkansas National Guard and sent in the 101st Airborne.

On September 25, 1957, a thousand armed soldiers escorted nine scared children back to school. The world watched. Raleigh schoolchildren, both black and white, watched in stunned silence from the sidewalk in front of Barclay's Radio and TV.

Raymond noticed one of the black kids eyeing him. He remembered him, Larry Something-or-other. Raymond had stumbled during a catch and fallen on him for the out. It took the coaches a little while to realize the players rolling on the ground at third base weren't hurt. They were laughing. Larry's team still won thirteen to seven that day.

When their eyes met in front of Barclay's, Raymond nodded toward the street. They stepped down off the curb together into a no-man's land between parked cars. Larry leaned on the trunk of a Buick and folded his arms. Finally, Raymond spoke.

"How's it going? You doing all right?"

"Yeah, I'm okay. What do you think about all that stuff happening down in Little Rock?"

"I'm glad it isn't happening here."

"You think it's not?"

"No, of course not. I mean, it isn't, is it?"

"What school do you go to?"

"East. Why?"

"And what school do I go to?"

"Douglass, I suppose."

"That's right. White schools get map names like North, East, South, and West. Mine got named after a slave. Why do you suppose that is? I say the folks here ain't doin' a whole lot better than Little Rock."

Tears welled up in Raymond's eyes. He looked away. "I guess I never thought about it. I mean, I'm sorry. I don't know what to say."

"Look, it ain't your fault, and it ain't my fault. We didn't do it. I'm only telling you how it is. You and me and all the rest of the kids in town are stuck with whatever mess the grown-ups got us into."

Raymond thought about that in silence.

Larry looked around, leaned in close, and asked softly, "You ever been inside the courthouse?"

"No, I guess not."

"Well, there's something there you ought to see."

The two boys slipped down the block toward the courthouse. Larry sat on the concrete wall in front and said, "I'm gonna stay here. I don't want no trouble. Just go inside and see for yourself."

"What? What am I going to see?"

"Act like you need to use the bathroom. When you come out, get a drink of water. Go on. What can happen? You're white. You'll be all right."

Raymond was bewildered. He found four bathrooms, each with little metal signs with letters stamped into them like license plates: "Colored Men," "White Men," "Colored Women," and "White Women." It took awhile to sink in. When he saw the water fountain, he bolted from the courthouse ashamed. Water was water. How could it be for "Whites Only"?

"Old-timers say they used to sell slaves here on the courthouse lawn. Strip 'em naked so people could see what they was getting. I figure folks around here ain't much different than Little Rock."

The two boys sat side by side on the concrete wall, trying to imagine what it was like. It was hard not to cry, and it was harder to know what to say. Finally, Raymond wiped his nose on the back of his hand and spoke.

"Larry, I don't want it to be like this."

"I don't either."

"Let's not be like them."

"Like who?"

"Grown-ups."

"Okay. Let's not."

Raymond pushed his bike along while they walked up Main Street, talking about Stan Musial and the Cardinals.

"It's not fair," Raymond said when they parted.
"I know," Larry answered.
"Stay safe. See you."
"You too."

Raymond climbed onto his bike and coasted downhill toward home. The neighborhood smelled of frying chicken and pork chops. He wondered why grown-ups sometimes acted like snapping turtles. They never stick their heads up until they run out of air. Then they grab a quick breath of air, take a hasty look around and sink back down to the bottom, pretending they are not there.

Chapter 3

▼

Dutch's Diner

Saturday, September 28, 1957

"Your office said I could find you here. Mind if I join you?"

Louis Baxter looked up from his lunch special to see a stunning redhead slide into the booth opposite him. He was slight of build, a bird-like man with long, bony fingers, a prominent Adam's apple, and the solemnity of an undertaker. Bacon and tomato dangled from his mouth, and he had mayonnaise on his chin. He slurped down his food and grabbed a napkin to mop up.

"Sure, I mean, no, I don't mind." He started to offer his hand, wiped it frantically with a fresh napkin, and tried again. "I don't believe I've had the pleasure ..."

"Do you call this running a newspaper?" she said, slapping down a stack of *Raleigh Journal-Messengers*.

"Now, hold on, Miss ... Miss ..."

"Millie. I teach English at the junior high school."

"I see, well, grammar and spelling errors occasionally get by us, but it is no call for a lecture from an authority on junior high English."

"Don't patronize me, you pompous windbag. I worked my way through college as a reporter for the *Kansas City Star*. I was there during the monopoly trials, and I'll put my experience and journalism degree up against yours any day. I'm not here about the *Messenger's* writing, although it sometimes misses the point. I am here to call you on your editorial policy. In a town this size, who else is going to do it?"

Baxter's eyes opened in astonishment. Flushing with rage, he took off his glasses and polished them with a napkin. Taking a deep breath to calm down, he leaned forward, put his glasses on the tip of his nose, and looked over them at her.

"Look here, young lady, this is hardly the time or the place for this kind of thing."

"Louis Baxter, you are not my father, so don't take that tone with me. There is no good time or place to tell an editor his paper panders to racial fear and hatred. You are scaring the crap out of the community. How's your circulation? Is advertising revenue up? And don't give me a load of baloney about the people's right to know. You and I both know that the newspaper game is won or lost on advertising sales."

He pushed away from the table so abruptly that he smacked the back of his head on the plywood booth. He looked around to see all eyes on him.

"She's right, you know," called the theater owner from across the room. "We had a fistfight in the lobby last night when some of the colored kids tried to sit downstairs. They got into it with one of my ushers. Popcorn everywhere. That never happened before. Gave 'em a refund and sent them back home. That stuff down in Little Rock has everyone jittery, and you sure ain't helping things much."

Dutch turned around from the grill, wiped his hands on his apron, and leaned on the counter. He was a big man, shaped like a bowling pin, with a hawk-like nose.

"Lou, you been coming in here for a long time now. Why do you suppose you mostly get to eat alone? Do you realize folks around here call you 'Bad-News Baxter'?"

Baxter sputtered, "I'll have you know I am not about to have my business run by a bunch of know-it-alls at the local greasy spoon!"

Dutch reared up, pointing two fingers at him like a gun. "If you plan to run a newspaper in this town, you might want to reconsider that policy. Now pay your tab, and get out of here."

"Well, Miss *Kansas City Star*, I hope you're satisfied. Look at the mess you made," he said as he threw his napkin down and slid out of the booth. Millie slid out in front of him, hands on her hips, head cocked to one side. She crowded him until he looked her in the eyes.

"Mr. Baxter, I came here to tell you that you have the opportunity of a lifetime. These are historic times. From what I see, the *Journal-Messenger* cranks out nothing but the latest scandal, hysteria off the AP wire, and one picture of a fatal car wreck a day. Is that all Potter knows how to shoot? Yet the *Journal-Messenger* could become the most important intellectual institution in this town. It's entirely up to you. Did you forget why you got into this business in the first place?"

He stepped around her, threw a wad of bills at the cash register, and stormed out, the door chime ringing furiously behind him. Millie sank back down to the booth and stared out the window. *How could it possibly have gone worse?* She felt a gentle touch on her shoulder and looked up to see Dutch with a cup of coffee.

"That was fun," he said, putting it down in front of her. "Lunch is on me. What would you like?"

Chapter 4

▼

Letter to the Editor

Monday, September 30, 1957

Dear Sir,

We live in historic times. Seldom has so much been demanded of our national leadership. Yet I question whether we are conscientiously equipping the next generation to lead. Two days ago, a youngster in my hearing asked his father to explain the conflict in Little Rock. The father's affection was apparent. He weighed the question carefully before kneeling down to say, "Son, you don't need to concern yourself with that." My heart goes out to that father, yet I wonder what might have happened had he said instead, "What do you want to know?"

Brave men and women have faced peril to secure the blessings we now enjoy, and we owe them a debt of gratitude. What better way to make good on that debt than to teach their descendants the difference between opinion, fact, and truth?

History will require wise and honorable citizens for tomorrow. To that end, I challenge the *Raleigh Journal-Messenger* to sponsor an essay contest open to all junior high and high school students in the Raleigh School District. Let each choose a topic about current events and tell us what it means to them. The *Journal-Messenger* can then print the winning entries to edify the whole community. Make no mistake. Our children are thinking about what they read and hear. What should concern us is what they are thinking. Why not ask them?

Sincerely,

Miss Margaret Millicent McKenna

October 4, 1957

On the first Friday in October, Russia startled the world by blasting Sputnik into orbit. The following Monday, a student brought Millie an envelope from the office. Anxious that she may have just been fired, she gave her students a reading assignment and opened the letter. Her hands trembled. Inside, she found a handwritten note under the *Journal-Messenger's* letterhead.

"What did you have in mind? L. Baxter."

CHAPTER 5

THE JOURNAL-MESSENGER

Friday, October 18, 1957

The clatter of the Linotype machine had finally stopped, and the galleys were done. The pressman would arrive at 5:00 AM to run the final edition of the Sunday paper. Lou Baxter stepped out into the freezing rain, pulling the collar of his overcoat up against the wind. He smashed his hat down on his head with one hand and turned to lock the office door. Footsteps crunched up the alley behind him. Startled, he wheeled to defend himself, the ring of keys left swinging from the lock.

"Mr. Baxter, it's me, Julius, Julius Gilmore."

"God almighty, Julius! You gave me a hell of a fright."

"I'm mighty sorry, Mr. Baxter. I shouldn't have walked up on you in the dark like that. But I didn't know how else to get to talk to you. I've been waiting in the car since I finished up. I need to ask you something mighty important. Have you got a minute?"

Lou looked at the icy street, then at the keys in the lock, and back into the earnest face of his janitor. Ice pellets slid down his neck, and he began to shiver.

"Julius, is this a personal matter or newspaper business?"

"Mr. B., d'you wants the truth?"

"Yes."

"It's bigger than that."

"Let's go inside out of this weather. We'll talk in my office."

Hanging his wet overcoat in the corner, Baxter slumped down into his chair and motioned for Julius to sit down. Julius had been in this office many times but always behind a mop. It felt strange to be here like someone with an appointment.

"Well, Julius, I'm listening. What's on your mind?"

"Sir, I've been working for you for a long time now, and mostly, I just try to stay out of the way 'cause I don't know nothin' about the newspaper business."

"Julius, are you asking for a raise? I rely on you, so let me give that some thought."

"No, sir. That's not why I'm here. In fact, when I gets through saying my piece, you may not want me to come around no more."

"I doubt you could say or do anything to make me feel that way, so why don't you say what's on your mind?"

Julius flicked melting ice off his cap and began to wring it with both hands.

"Okay, sir, here goes. It's about this essay contest. There are some powerful feelings loose in the community. Are colored kids going to be allowed to enter?"

"You know, Julius, I'm embarrassed to admit that I haven't given that much thought. The contest is open to any student in the Raleigh School District. Skin color is not a qualifier, so of course they can enter."

"Well, sir, that conjures up a whole lotta questions."

"How so?"

"My boys all went to Frederick Douglass through the eighth grade, but there ain't no high school for colored kids in Raleigh. The school board busses them over to Claremont. So can colored high school kids enter the contest or not?"

Lou pondered that question in silence and began to gnaw on his thumb. Julius twisted his cap between his hands and reckoned he had just lost a good job. He watched his boss stand, clasp his hands behind his back, and peer out into the night. The rain spit against the window. In time, he turned around, sat back down, and put his feet up on the desk.

"You know, Julius, you are a very wise man. We are talking about more than an essay contest here. We are talking about a social issue." He tapped his chin with one finger as he thought about it.

"How do you figure that, sir?"

"The problem is not with the rules of any contest. It's with the way things work around here. Maybe I need to do something to challenge that."

"I'm not sure I follow you."

"Julius, look. Three years ago, the Supreme Court outlawed separate-but-equal education. If the Raleigh school board can't think of a better solution than to contract with Claremont to teach your kids, then it seems to me they are still in the district. Because it's my paper and my contest, I can do what I think is fair. I say let them all enter."

"Well, sir, okay then. But here's the big question."

"What's that?"

"How can we be sure anybody will even read what the colored kids write? I mean, what's to keep folks from recognizing their names and just tossing their work in the ditch?"

"You didn't come here on your own, did you?"

"No, sir. The teachers at Douglass sent me to talk to you. They say, 'Why should we get the kids all fired up about this contest if it is going to go against them?' That's why I'm here."

Lou Baxter laughed out loud, dragging both hands through his hair. He waved at Julius to signal that he wasn't laughing at him.

"Mr. Gilmore, I'd say those are some pretty smart teachers. I want to hear what their students have to say. Let me think about this, and I'll tell you more in a couple of days."

Lou doodled on a tablet long after he heard Julius drive away, tires spinning in the sleet. He stared out the window at the miserable weather. It was getting late. He should go home. He glanced at the office clock. It was 8:45. He scowled at the strange new telephone squatting on his desk. He hoisted the handset to his shoulder, stuck his finger in a hole labeled "Operator," and spun the dial.

"Hello, Doris. Yeah, it's Lou Baxter at the *Messenger*. Can you connect me to Millie?"

"Jones, Elmendorf, McKenna, or Blackwell?"

"McKenna. She's the teacher, right?"

"Right. Lou, I can give you that number. You can dial her yourself now."

"Come on, Doris. You know I didn't want a damn dial phone in the first place. Just put me through, okay? Thanks."

Chapter 6

▼

The Contest

Wednesday, October 23, 1957
Raleigh Journal-Messenger

Essay Contest Rules: Let Every Voice Be Heard

Few things matter more than the truth, but it is tough to get by the bottle. Writing about it is like dropping stones down a well. A time comes when we must toss our ideas into the abyss and wait for a splash at the bottom. If the water is deep and we have written well, the sound is astonishing. The *Journal-Messenger* announces that our well is open to students grades seven through twelve in the Raleigh School District. Pick any topic from current events, and tell us what it means to you in 500 words or less. It's your turn to make a splash.

All entries must be delivered in a sealed envelope to the *Journal Messenger* during business hours between November 15 and 29 of this year. The entrant's name may not appear anywhere on the essay, but must be written, along with grade in school, on the front of the envelope. Entries bearing names will be disqualified. Submissions will be numbered in the order received. Envelopes and a master list will be kept in a secure location until judging is complete. Winners will be announced at the time of publication. All decisions by the judges are final. The mayor of Raleigh and members of the city council will judge entries on the basis of originality of thought and effectiveness of writing, not on the basis of agreement or disagreement with the author. Ladies and gentlemen, sharpen your pencils.

The first annual "Well Stone" contest received thirty-seven entries. The judges spent the better part of two weeks reading them over lunch at Dutch's Diner. They passed around folders sorted by grade levels and wrote their top three choices for each grade on an official score card.

Business became brisk at Dutch's, and more than one person was caught reading over a judge's shoulder. Somewhere along the way, a consensus arose. When all the judges finished a folder, it became available for the public to read. Dutch noticed a second wave of diners coming in after lunch. He even put up a cardboard sign as a reminder, "Judge by originality of thought and effectiveness of writing, not by whether you agree." Understandably, Dutch's became a public forum and the place for spirited debate. Most of it remained civil and good-humored.

The most popular subject was Communism and living under the threat of nuclear war with Russia. Eight students sought to make sense out of Sputnik and what would in time become known as the space race. A couple talked about Juan Batista and the future of Cuba, and a smattering of entries brushed up against race relations in the vaguest of terms. Only two contained thinly disguised bigotry. These were also the most poorly written because they elevated invective above intellect.

Some entries attempted to confront sleeping giants without awakening them. But one did more than trigger discussion. It prompted folks to make a side trip on their way back to work just to see for themselves. It was the sole entry in a folder marked "Grade 6, ineligible," but raised the biggest splash by far that year. The essay was entitled, "How Far Is Little Rock from the Raleigh County Courthouse?" by Larry Gilmore.

Chapter 7

▼

Paperboys

September 1959

It was a ritual. Every afternoon, the paperboys perched on the curb outside the office. They told lies while folding the newspapers stacked at their feet. The secret to an accurate backhand was the *Journal-Messenger* tuck. Like a Frisbee, it could be made to sail left or right. Speed and accuracy were everything. After all, none of them liked to lose time by dismounting to retrieve a paper from a hedge. It was always a race to claim the right stack, a race to fill the canvas bag, a race to mount up, and a race to hit the last porch before sundown.

"Boys, you are the face of the *Journal-Messenger*," Mr. Baxter often told them. "It's up to you. If you don't deliver, we might as well shut the doors. All our efforts fail, and you get docked for a miss. You are in the newspaper business now, so be polite and pay attention. Hit those porches and ride like the wind!"

Only a handful of boys lasted. For Raymond and his pals, who knew every yard and alley in town, it was easy money.

The older boys tormented them with tales of hazing freshmen, but it only hardened Raymond's resolve. His was not an intimidating figure. In fact, he was easy to overlook. There was absolutely nothing to warn the unwary that he could anchor himself to the earth and, with arms and legs flailing like broken springs, unleash a fury well beyond his weight and height. Raymond did not like to be pushed around. Confrontation made him feel nauseous, but he knew that sometimes, he had to fight. It was always when he least expected it.

"What's going on down there?" Wally said, pointing toward Main Street.

"I can't tell from here. Looks like trouble."

"Wanna cut across Sixth Street and stay clear?" asked Bud.

"Let's get a little closer first. I want to see what's going on."

From half a block's distance, they saw an elfish figure surrounded by a gang of boys. He was trying to protect his books and an instrument. Five kids a full head taller were picking on him. Raymond glanced at his pals, and all three rose onto their pedals to pick up speed. He reached into his basket for his Latin book.

"You are too a little freshman. Who do you think you're kidding? C'mon, pinky, get down on the ground."

"No, honest to God! I'm only in eighth grade. Let me go, please. I'll be late for violin."

"Oh yeah? Let's see what you've got in that case. Anyone here know where to stick a violin?"

Raymond jumped the curb and shot forward, swinging the book in a wide arc. Byron Donovan never saw what hit him. One moment, he was thumbing the latches on a violin case. The next, he was face down on the sidewalk, the left side of his head on fire, the knees of his Levi's torn and bloody. Before he could even roll over, a pair of hands grabbed him by the lapels, dragged him to his feet, and slammed him backwards into a tree. His head smacked the trunk so hard he saw double. He couldn't focus because his assailant was close enough to bite off his nose.

"Listen, moron, the next time you pick on a kid half your size, be ready to get your butt kicked all the way to China. I'll be coming for you."

Raymond drove an uppercut into Byron's solar plexus and watched him crumple to the ground, unable to breathe. He crouched down and leaned in close to his ear.

"I'm Raymond Thornton. I'm a freshman, and I don't like bullies. Get it?"

The Donovan kid gasped like a fish and nodded his head.

"You got anything to say?"

The kid shook his head and started to cry. His breath came in ragged gasps.

"Put the word out. It ain't a good year for hazing."

Raymond hesitated before rising. "Oh, yeah. Don't forget to turn me in. I want to tell somebody what you guys were doing."

He stood and turned to the other four.

"Who's next? Anyone else want some of this?" he said, picking up the book.

Wally and Bud had skidded in between the little kid and the others. They stood with fists ready. Four big kids were backing away from three smaller ones. The element of surprise had served them well, as had Raymond's surprising strength. They had just watched this kid toss Byron around like a rag doll. *Who is he?*

The seniors tried to act tough but backed away when Raymond advanced toward them. They gathered up their leader and backed slowly down the street, making empty threats. All Raymond cared about was that they were leaving.

He turned to see if the eighth-grader was hurt. The scrawny kid with big round glasses was piling up his books. Bud began picking up the things that had spilled from the violin case.

"You all right?" Raymond asked.

"Who, me? Yeah, I'm fine. I was just about to clean some clocks when you guys got here." He looked at Raymond and said, "Hey, if you had killed that guy, I'd never get to violin lessons."

He had long eyelashes, delicate features, and an impish grin. He wasn't a fighter, but at least he could joke about it.

"I'm Donny Weber. You swing a mean Latin book."

"What can I say? He was bigger than me."

"Who are you guys?"

"Raymond Thornton, and this here's Batman and Robin."

"Oh, yeah? Well, *e pluribus unum,* and all that kinda stuff."

"Bud Oswald. Today is my day to be Batman."

"Wally Grayson. I never get to be Batman. Where you going?"

"Down to pop's barber shop, across from the courthouse."

"Weber's, sure, I know where it is. I go there."

"Of course you do. It's the only one in Raleigh. Pop says his monopoly is the best kept secret in town. He only talks about it in the barber shop."

"Hey, c'mon. We'll walk with you."

It was only three blocks. They pushed their bikes. Donny was bright and very talkative. It was good the other boys didn't have much to say. He seemed lonely and desperate for friends—too desperate for Raymond. It was kind of creepy. Donny was the same age as Bud but seemed younger somehow. Anyway, it would always bother Raymond that he never got to know Donny better before he died.

CHAPTER 8

The Hanging

Wednesday, October 7, 1959

The quickest way to fold papers was to forget anything was printed on them. They were paid to deliver, not read. Raymond had folded a handful of papers before he noticed. Donny's picture was on the front page, in the top left corner. The photo was two years out of date, but there was still no mistaking him. The article stopped Raymond cold. He called out to Bud and Wally, and before long, they were all reading it.

Inquest Set to Look into Details of Boy's Death

Found Dead in Barn

Thirteen-year-old Donny Wayne Weber was found hanged last night in a barn at his family's farm two miles west of Raleigh on the Old Coal Mine Road, (Route B). An inquest will examine the circumstances of his death. Coroner Warren McHenry reported that death was due to strangulation. The inquest is awaiting a report from the State Highway Patrol Laboratory in Claremont, McHenry said.

The boy's father, Roger Weber, a local barber, found the body about 6:45 PM last evening. He and his older son Dillon Weber, 16, were searching for Donny with the help of a family friend,

Cecil Winters, 19. Donny's unclothed body was hanging from a rope tied to a brace at one end and thrown over a rafter. The boy's father said he immediately cut the body down and that Donny's hands were tied behind him. There was no evidence of a struggle or that anyone else was present.

The boy's parents arrived home with Dillon and his friend at about 6:00 PM. It was unusual to find the house locked and the family dogs inside. The three began searching. When Donny did not answer their calls, they went to the barn. Mr. Weber climbed up into the loft and found the body.

Donny was an eighth-grader in junior high. At school yesterday, he was reported to be in good spirits after making a presentation about jet propulsion in his last class. He left school at 2:15 and went to his father's barber shop on South Main Street, where he kept his bicycle, and rode home. He probably arrived home shortly after 3:00 PM.

Coroner McHenry estimates the time of death to be between 4:00 and 6:00 PM. Donny's clothes were neatly draped over a board in the loft. His shoes, socks, and the contents of his pockets were nearby, including a piece of paper containing class notes.

The father told Trooper L.D. Scanlon and Sheriff Randy R. Turner that Donny's hands were tied behind his back when he cut him down. The officers, assisted by Sergeant Fred Kramer of nearby Medina, found the boy's hands free but a piece of rope still looped around one wrist. Mr. Weber said he did not remember untying Donny's hands before calling authorities.

Investigators found a Boy Scout neckerchief nearby. Mr. Weber said it did not belong to his son. Dillon Weber later said it had been his but that he gave it to Donny.

City police went to the scene to help investigators.

Donny was born in Emporia, Kansas, on August 21, 1946, son of Roger and Lillian Weber. The family moved to Raleigh in 1949.

Funeral services will be held at 2:00 PM Saturday at St. John's Baptist Church here, the Rev. William Ludwig, pastor, officiating. Graveside services will be held at 2:00 PM on Sunday at the Emporia Cemetery, Emporia, Kansas. The body will lie in state at the McHenry Funeral Home until services here.

"Jeez, Louise!" Raymond whispered to Wally and Bud. "We've got to talk."

"No kidding. Let's go to Plan D after our routes are done, okay?"

"Okay."

Plans A, B, and C were to meet at a home according to birthday order. Plan D meant they needed neutral territory—the park. At this time of day, it also meant being late for dinner and getting in trouble at home, but not one of them cared. Donny was dead. They needed to talk first and then tell their parents the truth.

As night fell, the three boys found an empty pavilion and dropped their bikes near the fireplace.

"What do you think? Could it have been the seniors?" Wally asked.

Raymond couldn't talk. He had cried about Donny during his paper route and even now was choking back tears. They both looked at Bud. He was the detective.

"I've been thinking about that all afternoon, and I don't think so," Bud said after a moment.

"Why not?"

"A couple of them went out for football. By the time Coach gets done with them after school, they're too pooped to get into trouble."

"Raymond here just decked a football player?" Wally asked, pointing at their pal.

"Yep." Bud answered. "I figure that Donovan guy would rather catch up with him than Donny."

"Great." Raymond sniffed. "That makes me feel better. What do you know about him?"

"He's bad news," Bud answered. "Mom says his old man's in jail for trying to kill his mother with an axe handle."

"Jeez, nice family."

"That's nothing," Bud went on. "The Donovan kid shot him in the back to make him stop hitting her."

"did he get in trouble too?" Raymond asked.

"No, because if he hadn't, his old man would have killed her for sure."

"Oh, crap. He sounds like the kind of trouble that isn't gonna blow over."

"Not unless he gets himself locked up." Wally said. "And when you think about it that could happen any day."

"Let's hope it's sooner rather than later," said Raymond.

They sat in silence for awhile. Then Wally asked the big question.

"So what in the hell happened to Donny?"

Bud trailed a stick through the ashes in the fireplace as he thought. "We know what the reporter said, but that doesn't mean he got all of it right."

"Okay," Raymond said, "but Donny seemed pretty normal, don't you think?"

"Oh, sure. Just your normal four-eyed pipsqueak with a violin," Wally snorted.

Bud pushed his glasses up. "What's that supposed to mean?"

"Oh, jeez, I'm sorry. C'mon, you know what I mean, Bud. He was an easy target."

"It just doesn't make any sense," Raymond said.

"It does if someone had you at gunpoint." Wally pointed an imaginary gun at him. "Empty your pockets. Take off your shoes. Now take off your clothes."

Bud looked up from the ashes. "I'd try to stall for time, wouldn't you?"

"By hanging up your clothes?"

Bud shrugged. "First time for everything."

"Who would want to make it look like a suicide?"

"Somebody Donny trusted or who gave him no choice. Dillon maybe? I don't know. Who had motive, means, and opportunity?"

"How do you know all this stuff?"

"*Treasure Island* isn't the only book in the library, you know?"

"So now what?"

"We go home."
"And?"
"And wait until it's safe to check out the barn."

Chapter 9

▼

The Darkroom

Tuesday, October 13, 1959

When the last print came out of the fixer, Bud knew they had a problem. "Look at this, Ray. I don't know what to do about it."

"Let me see. Oh man, I see what you mean. The face tones are okay over here, but the black kids look like ink blots. We can't turn it in like this. Let's ask Mr. Hoff."

The photo paper couldn't handle the range of skin tones. They were up against the limits of black-and-white photography.

Mr. Hoff recognized it immediately. "This calls for some artful dodging. Do you boys know how to dodge?"

"What?"

"Come on, I'll show you."

He led them back into the darkroom and pulled out a cigar box. Inside were pieces of red film in various shapes and sizes. There were also several nine-inch-long wires coiled at one end to make a clasp.

"It's really kind of fun," Mr. Hoff said. He lifted out a wire and slipped a small red oval between the coils. He switched on the red lights and pulled the chain to kill the white one overhead. "Let's see what you've got."

Bud turned on the enlarger.

Mr. Hoff pointed and said, "The brightest spots are the darkest faces. Use the dodger to reduce the exposure, but keep it moving so you don't leave shadows." He held the red lens above the face and moved it in a small circle. "Think of it as painting with light."

"Wow. Okay, but how much?"

"That, my boys, is where the art comes in. You have to learn by trial and error. It'll require experimenting at first, but with practice, you'll get it right every time. Use scraps until you get a feel for it.

"Try to keep the dark faces together when you set up group shots. Otherwise, just make sure you have enough hands to do all the dodging. Try again and bring me your two best prints."

With that, he left them alone to master the art of the dodge. A few hours later, they pulled better prints out of the stop bath and transferred them to the dryer. No one realized it, but this was the start of Bud's career in crime-scene photography.

"What did you think about the inquest?" Raymond asked.

"Donny dies on Tuesday, and they rule on it on Thursday," Bud answered. "Seems pretty quick to me."

"Yeah, I know."

"What I don't get is why an undertaker is coroner in the first place. Knowing how to pickle 'em and plant 'em doesn't exactly make you an authority on homicide," said Bud.

"What are you getting at?"

"No one on the coroner's jury was a doctor or a cop. Donny gets a mortician, a trucker, and a bunch of good old boys from the Chamber of Commerce. They could figure out 'death by strangulation,' but after that, they were useless."

"What do you mean?" asked Raymond.

"A death certificate has check boxes for accident, suicide, or homicide. You know what they put down?"

"No idea."

"They typed in 'Open Verdict.'"

"As in, 'beats the hell out of me'?"

"Exactly. The coroner has officially declared, 'I dunno.'"

"Are you kidding?" Raymond asked.

"Man, I saw it. Mom works in the courthouse. I hang out there sometimes. You don't need to know any more than that."

"Well, hell, didn't anybody investigate?"

"That's the problem," Bud said. "Sheriff Turner is a hog farmer whose chief qualification is getting elected."

"The cops went over there, right?"

"Sure. But outside the city limits, the cops can't do a thing. Highway Patrol has labs and stuff, but it wasn't their case either."

"The paper made it sound like great police cooperation," said Raymond.

"Yeah, maybe, but that doesn't mean anybody actually processed any evidence. What's a country sheriff going to do but look around and say, 'Damn, it don't look like nobody else was in here, does it?'"

"Are you saying that nobody cares why Donny is dead?"

"Oh, I think they care, all right. They just don't know what to do about it."

"But they're grown-ups, for crying out loud!"

"Yeah, well, getting older doesn't make you smarter."

Raymond studied his friend. Bud's slumped shoulders suggested an aire of indifference, but one hand nervously fiddled with loose change in his pocket. The jingle of coins gave him away.

"You intend to go check out the barn, don't you?" Raymond asked. "The idea gives me the creeps."

"By now, any evidence is worthless. It's just that knowing the layout might explain what happened, that's all."

"Not me. I don't even want to go near the place."

"Yeah, okay, I understand. Let's drop it."

"You're going anyway, aren't you?"

"Naw. Guess not."

"Bud? Is Wally in on this?"

"Yes."

"Aw crap. When?"

"I was thinking over Thanksgiving break."

"Why then?"

"Gives us enough time to scout it out. Besides, I expect the family will want to spend Thanksgiving as far away from that barn as possible."

"Good point."

And so began the events that would eternally separate their lives into *before* and *after*—just as years are counted on either side of a life ending in a Roman execution in Jerusalem 2,000 years ago. One fateful day would determine which of them went to war, which did not, and how they shouldered that responsibility for the rest of their lives.

Chapter 10

▼

The Weber Farm

Friday, November 27, 1959

The two-story farmhouse sat back from the road about a hundred feet, a narrow gravel lane circling it. A large barn stood behind the house, once the pride of a working farm but now a sagging relic. Its tin roof had rusted out in places, and its siding weathered to the color of pewter.

No one had answered the phone at the Weber home all afternoon. Three kids on bikes rode slowly past the place looking for signs of activity. They saw neither cars nor fresh tire tracks on the frosty ground. That meant it was time to find the dogs.

Bud dismounted, hung his Nikon around his neck, and pushed his bike up the drive to lean it against a tree. Stepping onto the porch, he pulled open the screen and knocked on the front door. He found the dogs. Or, more accurately, they found him.

Growling and barking ferociously, they tore toward the front hall. Through a small window, Bud was startled to see a large black-and-tan mutt bouncing off the door, leaping, all bug-eyed with teeth bared, slinging saliva with every snap of his jaws. Bud slowly closed the screen door, collected his bike, and rode off in the direction of town.

In a way, he was disappointed that no one was home. It might be easier to explain that they were friends of Donny's, visit with Mr. Weber, and ask permission to look around. But that wasn't going to happen now. He glanced at his watch. It was almost four o'clock. Daylight would end soon. He found Wally and Raymond by a gate to a nearby pasture.

"Two dogs in the house, one big enough to be dangerous, but no one is home. Let's get going."

Bud and Raymond rolled their bikes into the field and hid them behind a clump of cedars. Wally slowly rode past the house to his lookout post, concealed his bike in the weedy ditch, and rolled under the barbed-wire fence. He dashed across an open field and crawled under the drooping boughs of a pine. Slithering forward far enough to see through the middle of the open barn, he checked the red lens on his scout flashlight and aimed a single flash. Bud answered with a single white flash. Wally saw Raymond's red light in the distance. It looked like he was beside the toolshed. With that, Bud went to work.

Each pop of a flashbulb inside the barn sent stray light splattering out through all the openings. It wasn't so noticeable in the daylight, but as the light failed, it became increasingly conspicuous. Pine needles in Wally's collar made his neck itch. Even lying on the cold ground, he sweated as he prayed that each pop of a flashbulb would be Bud's last.

On the opposite side of the barn, Raymond had his own problems. He thought he'd heard footsteps. A light breeze carried the sound of something moving from the cornfield along a shallow draw. He heard leaves rustling beneath the oak trees at the edge of the field, perhaps two people, maybe twenty yards out. It gradually became more distinct. He listened intently as they drew closer. He would soon be exposed.

He rose to his knees and twisted around to search. Nothing. Wait. There it was again. He eased into a crouch and began to back around the corner of the shed. The sound was closer now. He could hear them. He caught movement in the corner of his eye and spun to look. Two brown heads popped up in front of him. He stumbled, arms windmilling, and fell backwards. The deer snorted and wheeled, hooves pounding as they bounded away, white tails arcing in crisscrossing paths.

Raymond suddenly felt stinging in his flesh. Painfully, he rose to peel away blackberry canes, pulling barbs out of his skin and clothing. That was when he heard the approaching pickup. *Flashlight! Where the hell is the flashlight?*

He looked around for it frantically as the truck slowed and pulled into the drive. He dove back into hiding next to the toolshed, desperate to warn the others. In the distance, he could see Wally madly waving his red light at Bud.

Both pickup doors creaked open. As the first one slammed shut, a flashbulb popped in the hayloft. Silence settled over the farm for a moment, and then Raymond heard hushed voices.

"Pa, what was that?"

"Dillon, go get me the shotgun. Somebody's in the barn. Don't let the dogs out yet. Let me figure out what's going on."

The front door creaked open, and the screen slammed closed. Raymond saw Bud climb down the ladder and slink through the barn. He vanished into a stall and emerged from the doorway furthest from the house. Bud was going to make a run for it. He needed cover. The front door opened again.

Raymond stood up and hollered, "Mr. Weber, no! Don't shoot. It's me, Raymond Thornton! I can explain!" He stepped out into the yard between the toolshed and a pile of firewood. Startled, Mr. Weber wheeled and raised the shotgun to his cheek as he brought Raymond's upraised hands and horrified face into his sights. *What the hell?*

Bud sprinted for the nearest fence. The dogs burst from the door and launched off the porch after him. He dove for the top rail of the fence just as the black-and-tan intercepted him. Powerful jaws sank fangs through his tennis shoe into his toes, cutting his leap so short that he slammed down on top of the fence. Holding on to the top board with his arms and chin, he kicked blindly at the dog until he finally connected. The dog yelped, its teeth tearing free. Bud launched over the fence and landed in a shrieking heap. He grabbed his mangled foot with both hands. The dog rose with a shoe still in its jaws and began to give it the death shake.

As Mr. Weber swung the shotgun around toward Bud, a dark shape charged out of the barn, grabbed the muzzle of the gun, and slammed into his hip, driving him off his feet. Wally wrestled in the dark with a man who outweighed him by a hundred pounds. The muzzle flashed and a thunderous report deafened them all. Wally screamed and grabbed two bloody stumps on his right hand where his fingers used to be.

Suddenly, the yard light came on to reveal Mr. Weber standing over Wally waving the shotgun in his face. Without thinking, Raymond pulled a piece of firewood out of the stack and swung it like a bat into the man's ribcage, hearing the muffled crack of bones. Mr. Weber went down hard, moaning as he curled onto his side, and began to cough.

When Dillon stepped off the porch, Raymond picked up the shotgun and took charge. "Dillon, get your goddamned dog in the house, and go find the truck keys! We've got three people who need to get to the hospital now!"

Raymond tossed the shotgun aside, kneeled next to Wally, and tore off his own coat and shirt. He wrapped the shirt tightly around Wally's hand and told him to clamp down on it with the other as hard as he could. "You might need a tourniquet, but I'm not sure where to put it. I'll be back in a minute to see."

Dillon grabbed the dog by the collar and hauled him off toward the house. Raymond vaulted the fence. Bud was moaning and rolling back and forth, blood pouring from his foot. Raymond slid off his belt and cinched it tightly around Bud's ankle. He wrapped it several times and secured the free end with a half-hitch. Then, he hoisted his buddy up into a fireman's carry, clambered over the fence, and dashed for the pickup. Dropping the tailgate, he dumped Bud into the bed of the truck and turned to pull Wally to his feet. Wally stumbled to the truck in a crouch and sat on the tailgate, mashing his hands together between his knees. Raymond climbed up, grabbed Wally under the arms, and dragged him backwards toward the cab.

Dillon ran out of the house. "I can't find the keys. Pop, have you got 'em?"

"Unhhh. What?"

Raymond dropped out of the truck and knelt down beside him. "Mr. Weber, we need to get you to the hospital. Do you have the keys to the truck?"

He grunted, rolled over, and nodded toward his pocket. Raymond fished them out and handed them to Dillon.

"You drive, and I'll call the hospital."

"I don't know how!"

"Okay, then. Help me get your dad in the truck, and let's go. I'll drive."

"Can you handle a stick?"

"Sure. Just get it in second gear and leave it there. Hurry!"

The two boys loaded Dillon's dad in the cab. Dillon slid in after him. Raymond ran around to the driver's door and climbed in. He jammed on the brake, found neutral, and started the engine. Clutch down, he found reverse and eased the truck around in a semicircle. Finding second, he gunned the engine and slipped the clutch mercilessly until the truck lurched out onto the road and headed for town. Somewhere between the driveway and the mailbox, he found the headlights.

Mr. Weber muttered through clenched teeth, "What were you kids up to? You have anything to do with killing my boy?"

"God, almighty, no, sir! We were friends. We stopped the big kids from picking on him. We believed you when you said his hands were tied behind his back. The sheriff didn't do much, and it bothers the hell out of us. I guess we're angry too."

Donny's dad turned toward Raymond and began to weep. "Oh, my god! I nearly killed every one of you boys tonight. What's gotten into me?"

"Well, sir, for starters, somebody murdered your son. If that's not enough, I don't know what is."

Mr. Weber buried his face in his hands and began to sob. Dillon shot a couple of quick glances at his father and then stared at the floorboard, tears dripping off his nose.

The sheriff didn't question the dog attack but thought it odd that a visitor should fall and blow off a couple of fingers with Weber's twelve-gauge. Old man Weber himself seemed kind of iffy about where he was before he came running and fell over a stack of firewood. Sure, it was dark, but it also was his place. Didn't he know it was there? What really troubled him though was that all the stories matched. Everyone else bought the account in the *Journal-Messenger*.

Local Boys Rescue Three

> Neither Raymond Thornton, 14, nor Dillon Weber, 16, know how to drive. But that didn't stop them from getting three injured people to the hospital yesterday. Their quick thinking and teamwork led to the rescue of Bud Oswald, 14, from an attacking dog; Wally Grayson, 14, from an accidental gunshot wound; and Roger Weber, 52, from a possible punctured lung. The remarkable chain of events began when Thornton, Oswald, and Grayson called on the Weber farm yesterday to convey condolences over the recent death of their friend, Donny Weber …

Chapter 11

▼

Consequences

Later that night

It was late when Sheriff Turner arrived at the Thornton household. He had found Mr. Weber's shotgun, Bud's camera, and Raymond's coat at the Weber farm but missed the bikes. He sat on the couch, an oily cowboy hat on the pillow beside him. His Western boots and cowboy shirt seemed out of place, but the badge was genuine. Raymond's mother and father listened in silence while their son answered Sheriff Turner's questions. The sheriff had to go easy. He was just a kid.

"Why did you boys go out to the Weber place today?"

"You're not going to like my answer. Are you sure you want to hear it?"

"Go ahead, son."

"The newspaper article twice said Mr. Weber told you Donny's hands were tied behind his back. That means murder. Yet, in the same article, it said you found no evidence anyone else was there. We couldn't figure out how you could look around somebody else's barn and reach that conclusion, so we went out to see for ourselves. Sorry, but that's the truth of it."

Sheriff Turner flushed. After an ominous silence, he cleared his throat and went on. "All right. Tell me how all these people got hurt at the Weber place tonight."

"We went out there because of Donny. The Webers' dogs got out and took after Bud. Dillon brought the shotgun out of the house. Wally grabbed it but tripped, and it went off. Mr. Weber ran into a stack of firewood. Next thing I knew, there were three people injured, and Dillon and I were the only ones around to help them. He didn't know how to drive, so I did it. I don't have a license. Does that mean I am under arrest?"

Turner leaned forward and placed his elbows on his knees. He fiddled with his string tie and answered, "No, I don't plan to get laughed out of court for arresting a Boy Scout driving an ambulance without a license. But I'm telling you, Raymond, I don't take kindly to you kids meddling in my investigation."

"I understand that, sir. We didn't intend to interfere. We figured your investigation was over. The inquest is. Donny was our friend, and we can't just pretend he never existed. You were there. Was it suicide or homicide?"

"Frankly, son, I don't know yet. And even if I did, I'm pretty sure I wouldn't tell you."

"Well, okay. Now you know why we went out to see for ourselves."

Sheriff Turner could see he was getting nowhere. He glanced at his watch and stood. He collected his hat, shook Mr. Thornton's hand, nodded politely to Raymond's mother and excused himself. After seeing the sheriff out the door, Raymond's father locked up and came back into the room.

"Son, is there anything more about this you should tell us?"

This was the moment Raymond had dreaded. The boys had been trespassing, and two of them fought with Donny's father. The barber had threatened each of them with a shotgun. Maybe it was self-defense, maybe not. But if he told his folks, they would be drawn into the lie. He couldn't do that to them. But mostly, he couldn't tell them how it felt to look down the barrel of a shotgun. That scared the crap out of him.

"Dad, I don't believe there is any more I can tell you, except that the Webers don't need any more grief."

Raymond's father tilted his head and took a careful look at him. There was more to this story than he was getting. Yet there had always been a bond of trust between them. He decided the rest of the story could wait until Raymond was ready. He rose to place a hand on the boy's shoulder and look him in the eye.

"I'm proud of you for taking care of your friends today, Son. I didn't know you could drive a truck."

"I can't. I pretended it was Grandpa's tractor. We didn't have that far to go."

"Well, you did something today that folks will remember for a long time. Everyone will be watching to see how you handle it. Just remember who you are, and don't let us down."

"I promise, Pop. I'll never let you down."

Roger Weber was the first to leave the hospital, his collapsed right lung reinflated through the agony of a chest tube, his broken ribs taped tightly for support. Every breath reminded him how close he had come to killing more boys.

Before he went home, he visited Bud's room. Wally and Raymond were there. He entered wearing the same celery-colored pants and crumpled blue shirt he wore the night he was admitted. The laces on his brown shoes dragged the ground when he shuffled along because bending over was excruciating.

"Son, I have some good news. The rabies test on Poncho came back negative. You won't have to take the shots."

Bud went limp with relief.

"Nurse, do you suppose I could talk to these boys privately?" the barber asked. She closed the door behind her.

Mr. Weber, once tall and animated, now looked like an empty shell. He cleared his throat and looked down at the floor as he spoke. "You boys seem to be the only ones who care about my son, and I damn near killed every one of you. I can't tell you how ashamed I am. I will spend the rest of my life trying to forgive myself."

"Wait a second, Mr. Weber," Wally said, holding his bandaged hand above his shoulder to reduce the throbbing. "What we did was wrong. We had no business coming onto your place like that. It was our own fault. Thanks for not turning us in."

"Don't thank me. I could go to jail for the rest of my life. Boys, Lillian is falling apart, and I'm not far behind her. Dillon hasn't said two words to me since that night. Poncho was his dog. He's angry that he had to be killed to do the rabies test. If we stay in Raleigh much longer, I could lose what family I have left. We're leaving just as soon as we can."

"Gosh, where will you go?" asked Raymond.

"Probably back to Emporia. That's what I am thinking right now. But first, I need to ask you a favor."

"Sure."

"Anything."

"Don't be too quick to answer, not until you hear what I have to ask."

"Uhm, okay," said Raymond.

Mr. Weber searched their eyes one at a time before he proceeded. His whole body sagged. He had aged a hundred years since October, and it showed in his face.

"I want you to think about this real hard before you answer, okay?"

"Yes, sir."

"If you find out who did this to Donny …"

"Do you want us to call you and tell you?"

"No, I can't handle it right now."

"Yes, sir. We understand."

"I want you to make me a promise."

"What kind of promise?"

"Promise me that you will take care of it—yourselves. Do whatever it takes, but do it."

Raymond gulped. Bud pulled the blanket up under his chin, tears welling up in his eyes. Wally stepped forward and looked into Mr. Weber's face.

"You mean ... you're asking us to ... to kill somebody?" he said, the words swelling in his throat.

Mr. Weber held up one hand to break the eye contact.

"Son, I'm so upset I don't know what I mean. I just know that my boy is dead, and nobody else seems to care whether he gets justice. If you find out who did it, can you promise to do that?"

"Yes, sir," each one of them said.

And then he left.

"Did we just promise to kill someone?" Bud asked.

"No," Raymond answered. "We promised to see that Donny gets justice. That's different."

Chapter 12

▼

Raising the Question

Saturday, December 5, 1959

It wasn't that easy. The Webers' barn had never been properly searched; a dead boy lay beneath the soil of Kansas and with him, all bodily clues about his last moments. Those who found him had left town. To an outsider, it would appear that life in Raleigh remained unchanged. If it were not for two missing fingers and a boy on crutches, it could pass for a bad dream.

Miss Millie, now teaching high school, tried to help them catch up on their assignments. She couldn't get them to concentrate, so she offered to tutor them on Saturday at her home.

By suppertime, she was the only grown-up in Raleigh who knew what really happened that night at the Weber farm. What she heard broke her heart. She was their teacher not their mother, so she could not take them in her arms and comfort them. However, she ached for them all the same. So she played the piano, and they talked. Her eyes were red and puffy when she led them onto the porch to say good-bye.

"Boys," she said, gently touching a shoulder here, a cheek there, "you are too young to know about all this. Thank you for telling me. Let me think about it. There must be something we can do. Go home now. Eat supper. And sleep knowing that you must turn Donny over to God. He is the only one who can help him now."

"No, ma'am, he's not. We aren't done yet," Raymond answered her. She smiled at him, her eyes glistening with tears.

They each gave her a timid hug before leaving. As they approached the gate, Wally bumped Raymond off the sidewalk. All it took was a little horseplay for them to become boys again. Millie went inside and climbed the stairs to her bedroom. She stepped inside and closed the door softly. Then she crossed to the rocker by the dormer window, stared out at the setting sun, and wept.

The next morning, while dressing for church, a sense of peace settled over her. She knew what had to be done. After school on Monday, Miss Millie told the boys about her idea.

"It has to be genuine. You can't lay it on too thick," she said. "If you get the tone right, only two people will know, and they will be completely helpless to do anything about it. Then, you wait for others to spring the trap. Do you understand?"

"Yes, ma'am. I think I can do that," Raymond said. "Let me work on it tonight, and I'll show it to you tomorrow."

He was the logical choice to write the essay. Bud's mother could get fired for letting him see Donny's death certificate. Wally still had to figure out how to hold a pencil in his injured hand. It was all he could do to turn in legible homework. Raymond had one other advantage: He understood that 500 words was a limit, not a goal. He was content to stop when his thoughts were complete, not when he hit a magic number.

In Praise of Local Law Enforcement

> It is essential to acknowledge the contribution local law enforcement officers make to our community. The blessings of social order we enjoy in Raleigh are a direct result of their quiet and efficient work. Our local police officers and the county sheriff's department are on the front lines of this effort.

> Life in a small town provides many opportunities to know the local citizens individually, and that contributes to efficient law enforcement. A recent tragedy serves as a case in point. Last October, a local boy met an untimely death under questionable circumstances. In what could serve as a model of interagency cooperation, officers from the Raleigh Police Department, the State Highway Patrol, a special investigator from Medina, and Sheriff Randy Turner worked together on the case. The sheriff provided the county coroner with the results of his investigation. The coroner's jury completed the inquest into the boy's tragic death only two days later. By comparison, closing such a case in a major metropolitan area like Memphis, St. Louis, or Kansas City might take months, or even years.
>
> One of the unrecognized contributors to our local law enforcement community is the county coroner, who conducted the inquest to determine the manner and cause of death. Who could possibly serve better in that capacity than Warren McHenry, a licensed mortician who deals with the deceased every day? We are indeed fortunate to live in a community where professional law enforcement is joined with the best efforts of civic-minded volunteers. Everyone involved in this case should be commended for getting to the bottom of the matter so quickly.

His initial draft was 269 words, but Raymond felt he had made his point. When he showed it to Miss Millie, she suggested he submit it just as it was. Perhaps its brevity would draw favorable attention. Neither of them was prepared for it to receive an honorable mention in the Well Stones contest.

The essay became a point of pride in the community. The sheriff received daily congratulations for his fine work, and compliments even got back to the coroner. Yet both men grew uncomfortable because of the public attention. The reason would become obvious in the weeks to come.

In the last days of 1959, a letter arrived at Louis Baxter's office urging the *Journal-Messenger* to look into Donny Weber's inquest. It made an interesting suggestion: After examining Donny's death certificate, perhaps Mr. Baxter should visit with the paperboy who wrote the essay about it. The letter described the article as a "sacrifice bunt" and said the author would explain. It was signed by Miss Margaret Millicent McKenna.

An unusual group gathered at the Thornton residence on New Year's Eve. Naturally, Wally and Bud, semipermanent residents in the Thornton household, were there. Lou Baxter and Miss Millie arrived at seven o'clock.

While the sheriff's deputies and local police were busy looking for drunks and holiday mayhem, no one noticed a small party gathering to welcome the next decade. Raymond's mother served her famous mincemeat pie and coffee. The boys consumed their pie, along with a half gallon of milk, in the kitchen.

After pie and pleasantries, Millie brought the meeting to order in her own fashion.

"Mr. and Mrs. Thornton, the boys have told me the full story about the night they went to the Weber farm. It differs significantly from the published story. They want to tell you about it tonight. It may seem alarming at first, but when they finish, I am confidant you will regard their decisions as highly as I do."

"Call us Sylvia and Reggie," Mrs. Thornton said.

Raymond's father said, "I suspected all along there was more to it. Thanks for looking out for them."

"You're welcome. They are good kids. Lou, did you get to look at the death certificate?"

"Yes, I did."

"And?"

"The inquest was a sham."

"What do you mean?" asked Sylvia.

"The death certificate reveals that nobody has the foggiest notion how Donny was hung. Instead of choosing between accident, homicide, or suicide, McHenry typed in 'OPEN VERDICT,' in all capital letters."

"So it's an open case?" asked Mr. Thornton.

"Well, yes and no, Reggie. According to the death certificate, that may be true, but my sources in the sheriff's department tell me that he is not pursuing it. In fact, he has buried the file somewhere."

"Reggie, Sylvia," Millie said, "that's why the boys went out to the Webers'. But you need to hear the whole story from them. Lou, take notes. The boys want you to."

Reggie went into the kitchen. "Hey, guys, we're ready for you to tell us what really went on at the Weber place."

They followed him back into the living room. Wally carried a magazine. Bud eased himself into the rocking chair and leaned his crutches against the lamp table. Wally sat Indian-fashion on the floor with Raymond next to him.

Bud cleared his throat and said, "This all started when I happened to see the death certificate at the courthouse where Mom works. I realized then that the sheriff had blown it. He said that there was no evidence that anyone else was there. Yet, according to Mr. Weber, Donny's hands were tied behind his back. Mr. Baxter, that was in the newspaper article twice."

"I know. I wrote it. The man told me the same thing."

"Did you go inside the barn?" Bud asked.

"No. The body was still in there, so I didn't go in."

"Well, I did, the night after Thanksgiving. And I took pictures. The place is piled high with old tractor parts and junk and clutter. I even went up into the hayloft. The floor is covered with straw, so I doubt there were even footprints. There is just no way in hell Sheriff Turner could tell if anyone else had been in that barn. Sorry, Mrs. Thornton. Wally, show them the pictures."

Wally slid a stack of eight-by-ten photographs out of a *Life* magazine with a picture of Eisenhower on the cover. He was waving to a crowd in Pakistan. Wally spread the black-and-white prints out on the coffee table. The Thorntons leaned forward to study them, and Mr. Baxter stood up to look over their shoulders.

The boys told them everything. Raymond's parents listened intently, but that did not mean they were pleased. Once the boys had finished, Lou referred to his notebook and walked them through it again in chronological order. When he was satisfied, he asked Raymond another question.

"Do you mean to tell me you deliberately wrote that baloney, knowing all the time it was a lie?"

"Yes, sir, but if you reread it carefully, you will see that none of it was a lie. When I asked who was better qualified to be coroner, that's what I meant. There surely has to be someone who is better qualified than a guy who runs a funeral parlor. And when I said that everyone involved in the case should be commended, that's what I meant. They *should* have done the kind of job that gets them a medal, but no one in this bunch did. Besides, who is going to listen to us if we say the sheriff is a bum and the coroner is incompetent? We're just kids. Instead of tackling them head on, I put the spotlight on them. This way, when it all comes out, it will be handled by grown-ups, not just a couple of kids griping about the sheriff."

"And you expect the *Journal-Messenger* to do your dirty work for you?"

"No, sir," Raymond answered. "We expect you to publish the facts. That's all Donny deserves."

"That's an interesting notion coming from somebody who fed us a phony story." Lou looked at Millie. "What did you mean when you said the essay was a sacrifice bunt?"

"That's how Wally described it, but I'm not sure I can explain it. Wally?" Millie said, looking over at him.

"Sometimes it is better to get a teammate on third, even if you get thrown out at first," he explained. "Nobody scores without crossing third base. A bunt is a safer bet than a home run. Make 'em chase all over the infield."

Lou thought that over. He did not like publishing a false version of events, but it certainly wasn't the first time. He admired the boys for honoring a promise to Donny's father. They were not out for glory. He let out a sigh and looked over at the Thorntons.

"What do you folks think?" he asked.

A glance passed between them, and Reggie Thornton spoke. "Lou, I don't think I could tie my own hands behind my back. Can you?"

It would seem Miss Millie had a knack for encouraging others to do the right thing, even newspaper editors.

Chapter 13

▼

The Power of the Pen

Monday, January 4, 1960

When school started again on Monday, Miss Millie stood in front of her freshman class to make an announcement.

"Ladies and gentlemen, last semester, we studied the parts of speech and diagrammed sentences. This semester, we will use what we have learned to write an essay."

Ignoring the groans, she continued, "To do this, Mr. Randolph and I will work together. You will read the newspaper each day in civics class and discuss current events. From that, you will select a topic that interests you and begin to develop your own point of view. Does anyone know what I mean by that?"

No one did, or at least no one volunteered.

"People don't want to read warmed-over news. It's boring. Instead, a reader's curiosity is aroused when a writer finds a unique way of looking at an issue or asks a new question. A good essay challenges the reader to think, maybe even question his own beliefs. Does that make sense?"

Heads bobbed in agreement around the room.

"This semester, you will start an essay for the *Journal-Messenger* contest. Don't worry if it's not perfect by the end of this semester. It will only be the first draft. When summer is over, we will look at it again with a fresh eye and polish it for the contest. Any questions?"

"Yes, ma'am." It was Sue Fletcher. "How soon do we have to choose our topic?"

"That's a good question. I want you to start writing by the end of next week, even if you decide later to change topics. Writing is mental exercise, not a mechanical process. To be good, it must be something you care about. Many times, writers start a project only to chuck it when something better comes along."

Raymond's hand went up.

"Yes, Mr. Thornton?"

"Did you just tell us to start out writing without knowing where we're going?"

"Exactly. Think about it. In science, how many discoveries were accidental? Madam Curie didn't start out to discover radium. She just wanted to know why some stuff glows in the dark. Jonas Salk didn't start out to find a cure for polio. He wanted to learn why the influenza epidemic of 1918 was so devastating."

"Aren't those just exceptions, though?" This came from the back row. It was Andy Smallwood. What was he doing asking a question?

"Not at all, Andy. Penicillin was discovered because of a sloppy laboratory. A guy named Fleming finally cleaned out a bunch of moldy Petri dishes when he noticed something had killed a bunch of staphylococci. Science is creative. It is often accidental discovery. Did the Wright brothers fly on their first attempt? Why should writing be different? Do you understand?"

"But shouldn't we pick a really good topic before we start out?" Wally asked.

"Ah, leave it to Mr. Grayson to bring us to the point. 'Why put out any effort until we find the perfect topic?' Wally, writing isn't like baking cakes by using the same recipe over and over. It's a skill just like hunting, drawing, driving, or playing ball or an instrument."

"I was afraid of that."

"How did you get to be a good base runner?"

"By playing ball."

"There you go. Look, without starting on the first thing, a writer might not recognize a better subject when it comes along. It's an organic process. It's not like pouring concrete. A cement truck churns all the way to the job site. Then it dumps big globs of concrete down a chute into some ready-made form. Chunk it down, smooth it out, dress the edges, and what do you get? A slab of concrete. Have you ever heard anyone say, 'Oh, my! What a beautiful slab of concrete?' The writing process is more like being lost in the woods. When you are lost in the woods, you get hungry. Then what?"

"You start eating stuff."

"Right. First some leaves, maybe some bark, and then you discover berries. How do you figure out you like berries more than bark?"

"By comparison?"

"Thank you, Wally. I rest my case. Your idea may change several times. That's okay. Just turn in a journal of your work by the end of this semester.

"The first rule is that writing is rewriting. The second is this: It is impossible to write well about something that doesn't matter to you. So be honest with yourself. Look for the surprise. Anyone here object to improving your mind?"

On Thursday, January 14, Lou Baxter published an editorial entitled, "The End of Innocence," in which he suggested that Raleigh's purity ended with the botched investigation of Donny Weber's death. He exposed the "open verdict" on Donny's death certificate.

> Ours is a wonderful community, but it is time to admit that God does not keep us under a glass bowl to shield us from harm. An imperfect world surrounds us. Its evils stalk us up and down the streets of Raleigh. The time has come for law enforcement in this county to embrace forensic science, particularly in suspected cases of violent crime. We need access to a medical examiner qualified in

forensic medicine. As a community, we cannot allow any more of our children to die under undetermined circumstances.

In certain quarters, Randy Turner became known as Sheriff "Turnip" for having just fallen off the truck. For him, hog farming regained its allure. The coroner didn't help. McHenry complained that his findings were hampered by the inconclusive investigation. The sages at Dutch's Diner began to doubt whether an undertaker had the training to do autopsies. It was a bleak time for Turner and McHenry.

Understandably, Miss Millie's freshman English class struggled with the assignment. They were accustomed to structure, not thinking. But bit by bit, the discussions in civics class began to bear fruit. The students started looking forward to reading the paper in class and to discussing what they read.

The news of 1960 provided ample opportunities. On February 1, Black residents of Greensboro, North Carolina, held a lunch counter sit-in to end segregation. Between February 14 and 28, all eyes were on the Winter Olympics in Squaw Valley, California. A Slovenian ski jumper named Vinko Bogataj, while hurtling down the ski jump, fell just before his leap into the sky. Footage of his body cartwheeling through the crowd soon came to symbolize "The Agony of Defeat" on the *Wide World of Sports*. G. D. Searle Company introduced Enovid, the first birth control pill. A House committee investigated radio pay-for-play, called "payola." Dick Clark, the DJ on American Bandstand, had to testify.

Writing was not easy for Wally because of his injured fingers. Besides, he was more interested in Betty Ann Milton. Bud and Raymond threw themselves into it with greater enthusiasm. However, it was not until May 5 that Bud found his topic.

Russia Shoots Down U.S. Plane; Warns of Retaliation

… The State Department report said a single-engine, high-altitude jet used in weather research took off from Adana, Turkey, with a civilian pilot and has been missing since. The disappearance of the plane was announced last Tuesday.

"During the flight of this plane," the report said, "the pilot reported difficulty with his oxygen equipment.

"It is entirely possible that having a failure in the oxygen equipment which could result in the pilot losing consciousness, the plane continued on automatic pilot for a considerable distance and accidentally violated Soviet airspace."

On May 7, Kruschev revealed the Soviets had recovered not only the aircraft, but also the CIA pilot named Francis Gary Powers. The chairman described him as being "alive and kicking." Bud was perplexed.

If the aircraft had oxygen equipment, it must have been essential for the pilot. It would take time to enter Soviet airspace. There seemed to be a contradiction. How, he wondered, could a pilot survive an oxygen failure that allowed the aircraft to stray "*a considerable distance*" into Soviet airspace?

"Hey, Ray," Bud asked as they walked home from school, "if I were a map of the Soviet Union in this town, where would I hide?"

"Oh, jeez. What are you up to now?"

"I'm thinking about the 'Stones' contest. Did you ever hear of a place called Sverdlovsk?"

"What?"

"Sverdlovsk. S-v-e-r-d-l-o-v-s-k. It's in Russia somewhere."

"Naw. Why? You wanna go there?"

"I don't think you can get there from here without a U-2."

Raymond stopped. He had seen Bud like this before, thumb hooked in his jeans, hunched forward, like he was searching the ground for clues. Bud felt Raymond stop and turned to look. Their eyes met. They understood each other.

"You're serious, aren't you?"

"Not necessarily. Just thinking, that's all," he said with a shrug.

"Yeah, sure! I've seen you think before. Last time, it got people hurt."

"What do you know about oxygen systems?"

From the corner of Eighth and Business Route 19, Raymond looked to his right past Goofy Gil's gas station toward home. He looked to his left toward town.

"We're going to the library, aren't we?"

"I dunno. If you want to, I guess. Just don't tell anyone, okay?"

"Oh, don't worry. I'm not going to say a word. But I'm getting that creepy feeling again."

"Aw, blow it out your tailpipe. You love it, and you know it."

"Well, that's true. So what's the deal?"

By the end of the semester, Bud turned in his journal, but, just as Miss Millie predicted, it was only the beginning of an idea. He got an A and spent a lot of his summer in the library. He became convinced it was all a lie. Kruschev had caught the U.S. spying.

When his Dad got the phone bill in July, he blew his top.

"Bud, who the hell called Seattle? Was it you?"

Bud swallowed. "Oh, that. I called Boeing. A 707 can go up to 40,000 feet. Mostly, they fly at 35,000 or below. They pump air into them so it feels like 8,000 feet. And the pilots have to be ready to grab oxygen masks in an emergency."

"Well, gee, ain't that just swell! And explain to me again why I should pay twenty bucks for that?"

"Pop, you don't have to. I'll pay it. I have some money saved up."

"Son, what's this all about? And why didn't you ask for permission?"

"You wouldn't let me call, would you?"

"No."

"That's why," Bud said with a grin. "Look, I have this idea for the 'Stones' contest about Francis Gary Powers. You know, the U-2 pilot?"

"Okay, hot stuff. Just what do you know about him?"

"I know his plane went down thirteen-hundred miles inside Russia at a place called Sverdlovsk. They caught him. He bailed out. That means he was alive at least two hours after they say he lost oxygen. That can't be, Pop. Air force guys go to 25,000 feet in an altitude chamber. They pass out about a minute after taking off their mask. If somebody doesn't put it back on them, they die. So either this guy's body should be in the wreckage, or the oxygen thing is a lie."

"Really?"

"Yep. It's all hokey. The only thing I can find on the U-2 is a picture put out by NASA. It's a goofy-looking thing, like a glider, but with a jet engine. So I called Boeing to get an idea what it takes to keep this pilot guy alive at extreme altitudes. Take it from me, Pop. This deal is all wrong. At least, that's what I'm working on right now."

Later that night, Bud's mother and father were watching the ten o'clock news when his father recounted the conversation with Bud.

"Can you believe it, Gloria? The kid just calls Boeing in Seattle. Cost me twenty bucks."

"Did he pay you back?"

"Well, yeah. But he didn't even get permission first."

"Larry, what is really bothering you, the money, or the fact that Bud knows you well enough not to ask?"

"Ouch. That smarts."

"Look, honey," she said, putting down her crocheting, "stop and think about how his mind works and tell me it doesn't make you proud. Were you like that at his age?"

Mr. Oswald grinned at her. "Okay, you win. This calls for ice cream. Can I bring you some?"

"Millie, what happens now?" Lou Baxter asked in one of their frequent phone calls. "The publicity has been good for the *Journal-Messenger*, but I feel like I'm trying to run a business in a goldfish bowl. You talked me into this. Do you have any good ideas how to get me out?"

"The answer is obvious, Lou. We don't shut it down; we let it grow! Let's turn it into a summertime writing festival and open it to anyone.

But you have to be present to win. The *Messenger* can trigger a cultural and tourism boom in Raleigh. We get noted authors to conduct workshops. We bring in publishers looking for new talent. And we fill up the Royal Hotel. What do you think?"

"Holy cow, Millie! I'm buried as it is. I can't take on any more."

"Oh, Lou, I don't mean you. I mean the Chamber of Commerce. Turn it over to them. Isn't that just the kind of thing they are looking for?"

By the summer of '62 the courthouse square blossomed with awnings. Colorful umbrellas stood in the sunshine above street vendors and sidewalk cafés. Raleigh looked like a Norman Rockwell painting from the *Saturday Evening Post*.

Meanwhile, history provided plenty to write about. In 1961, Yuri Gagarin became the first man in space. A CIA-backed invasion of Cuba collapsed at the Bay of Pigs. Alan Shepard spent fifteen minutes in space. In a speech, President Kennedy said, "Every prudent family should have a bomb shelter." Ernest Hemingway committed suicide with a shotgun. And overnight, Russia raised the Berlin Wall, thereby proving Winston Churchill right about the Iron Curtain.

The news contained plenty of fodder in 1962 as well. John Glenn made three orbits around the earth. Kennedy and Kruschev went eyeball to eyeball over the Cuban Missile Crisis. Kruschev blinked. A U-2 took the pictures that started it all. And, on a bridge over the Havel River between Potsdam and Berlin, the U.S. swapped KGB spymaster Rudolf Abel for Francis G. Powers. The Well Stone Writing Festival was born.

Chapter 14

▼

Physical Education

September 1960

There wasn't anything intrinsically wrong with PE. Raymond had always loved sports, so the workouts weren't the problem. His problem was a second-year senior with a head like a pumpkin. At six feet two, two hundred and twenty-six pounds, sporting a turned-up collar, duck's-ass haircut, scraggly mustache, Camels in his shirt pocket, and a long memory, Byron Donovan had made it his life's work to get even with Raymond for clocking him with a Latin book.

Raymond was on his own. Bud and Wally had PE second hour. They were showered and off to their next class before Raymond even hit the stairs to dress out. His primary strategy was avoidance.

He always chose one of the lockers close to the coaches' office. He didn't strip until Byron hit the showers, and he took whatever circuitous route would steer him away from the bully. If Goliath wanted to start something, it had to be obvious. And David would have to change tactics.

It didn't take long to figure out why Donovan was never a starter on the football team. It was the same reason he was repeating his senior year. Not only was he a poor scholar, his speed and coordination were lacking. So he used his size to make up for his cowardice. Raymond stored that information away for later use.

In the second week of school, Donovan hid outside the shower and waited for Raymond to come out. The crack of the towel on the smaller boy's flank sounded like a firecracker. Raymond spun his towel into a rope and took two quick shots at his assailant's crotch. Donovan doubled over and started backing away, hands out to fend for his private parts. It left him open for the shot Raymond was really looking for—the left eye. With one crack, Donovan was on the floor screaming, curled in a tight ball, his left hand protecting his groin and his right shielding his face.

"What in the Sam Hill is going on out here?" Coach Mertz bellowed as he charged out of his office.

"He started it, Coach. I finished it," Raymond said, turning to show the flaming red welt on his left buttock. "You ask anyone here."

Coach didn't have to ask. Everyone started talking at once.

"All right, all right!" he said waving his arms. He knelt down by the big kid.

"Where did he get you?"

"My eye! My eye!" Byron wailed.

"Take your hand away, son, so I can see."

Coach peeled Donovan's trembling hand away to expose an angry purple mark that ran from the outside corner of the eye back toward the ear.

"Jesus, Thornton! You could have put his eye out!"

"Exactly, Coach. I could have. But I didn't. This is his last warning. It's not a fair fight because this baboon outweighs me by sixty pounds. The next time he jumps me, I will use a brick."

It was the first time Raymond had been sent to the principal's office for discipline. Mr. Diener apparently knew Byron well. He started chewing him out in the main office.

"Donovan, when are you going to start picking on somebody your own size?"

"But, Mr. Diener, everyone here is smaller than me."

"You big lummox!" Diener roared in fury. "What do I have to do to get through to you? Do you want to get expelled? Is that what you're after? Do you understand that nothing would please me more? Go, get in my office, and sit!"

Mr. March, the assistant principal, took Raymond into his office and closed the door. He tried a different approach.

"Raymond, you're a good kid. Everyone around here likes you. But this is going to be a black mark on your record. The rules are the rules. If you brick Donovan, you're out. Do you understand?" That was how Brick Donovan got his name.

Brick had the wisdom to let things cool off. But he never forgave and was slow to forget. The day came when Raymond and Brick were on opposing sides in a game of dodgeball. Brick and his teammates were the shirts and Raymond's side the skins. Donovan ran Raymond down several times and nailed him.

Soon, Raymond baited Brick into another rundown. But this time, Larry Gilmore passed him a basketball. Raymond wheeled, planted his feet, and snapped the ball with both hands straight at Brick's face. The bully's head snapped backwards, but his feet kept going. He hit the floor spread out like a snow angel and didn't move.

Coach Mertz blew the whistle and called time-out. He walked over to Raymond, planted his fists on his hips, and glared at him.

"Goddamn it, Raymond. What the hell do you call that?"

"Self-defense, Coach. Self-defense," Raymond said turning to show the big red welts on his side and back. "What were you gonna do? Just stand there and let him keep going? If you don't stop him, I will."

"All right, Thornton. That's enough. Hit the showers and get out of here before he comes to. This palooka's gonna have one hell of a headache."

Mertz sent a couple of kids for a wet towel and smelling salts. He squeezed water into Brick's face and mopped it with the towel. The boy stirred, but his lights were still out. The smelling salts worked. The instant the capsule snapped under his nose, he sat bolt upright, shaking his head to clear the fog.

"Where is that little shit? I'm gonna kill him."

Coach hissed, "Watch your mouth. You're not gonna kill anybody today, so shut up and listen." He waved the other boys off to the locker room. When the last one was out of sight, he grabbed the front of Donovan's shirt, pulled him into his face, and whispered, "Listen to me, you little punk! You got exactly what you deserved. You are one helluva slow learner. So let me make this plain to you. If you're gonna get to Thornton, you're going to have to whip me first. And when I get done with you, you'll sound like Minnie Mouse. Now get your sorry ass up off my gym floor and go take a shower."

Three weeks later, Coach Mertz stepped out of his house to find his car ablaze, its windows shattered and flames leaping into the trees overhead. The next half hour was a blur of sirens and firemen fighting to contain the damage from the exploding gas tank. When at last they extinguished the burning tires, the damage totaled one car, four trees, and three spans of ruined cable.

On March 13, 1961, the *Journal-Messenger* ran an article about a race riot in the Missouri State Penitentiary. An inmate named Wilmer "Butch" Donovan, who was white, had been overpowered in the cafeteria by two black inmates and stabbed repeatedly. A fight broke out along racial lines, and before the guards got it under control, a number of inmates had died. Butch Donovan was one of them.

Few in Raleigh even noticed the article, let alone made the connection. But that was not how Brick Donovan perceived things. He was convinced that the death of his father at the hands of "a coupla nigger convicts" was the talk of the town. Someone had to pay. He turned his attention to Larry Gilmore, "Raymond Thornton's pet nigger." He found his opportunity in the last week of April during the PE softball tournament. Coach had concluded that the best way to keep Raymond and Brick from having another go at each other was to put them on the same team—separated by a great distance. Donovan was playing third base and Raymond was in right field when Larry Gilmore hit a double.

Larry was fast and aggressive, so it was no surprise to see him take a big lead off second as the pitcher stepped into his windup. A line drive into right field was his signal to go. Raymond scooped the ball up on the bounce and fired it off to Brick at third base in an effort to head off the run. Brick took two short strides towards the pitcher's mound to catch the ball and wheeled to see Larry launching in a headlong dive for the bag. Brick sidestepped quickly and came down on Larry's outstretched arm as hard as he could. But that was not enough. He then took a short step back to deliver a powerful kick in the ribs—again and again.

Raymond watched the world slip into slow motion. The moment he fired the ball to Brick, he knew something terrible was about to happen. Brick's face was a study in demonic concentration, the tip of his tongue lolling at the corner of his mouth.

No sooner had Raymond released the ball than he sprinted after it. He watched Larry launch into a graceful arc. He saw Brick wheel and time his strides carefully to plant his right foot on Larry's left forearm with all his weight. The face of shortstop Dennis Rothstein, standing flat-footed with his mouth agape, bobbed past him with each stride. He watched Brick haul his leg back to deliver a kick to Larry's ribs. His legs pumped faster. He watched the next windup and the second kick, followed by a graceful little hop into a dropkick to the head. Raymond dove for Brick's knees as his right foot began its arc toward Larry's face. He hooked the swinging ankle with his right arm, drove his head between Brick's legs, and threw his left shoulder against the inside of Brick's left knee. He heard the snap of bone and the crunch of cartilage, felt the leg buckle, and knew before he hit the ground that Brick's knee had disintegrated. A human leg doesn't bend that way.

He tumbled and rolled away and became aware once again of sound. The ball field reverberated with Brick's howl. First, an echo came back from the shop building, then from the yellow brick walls of the junior high wing, and again from the distant gymnasium.

That moment changed the future. By the end of the school year, Coach Mertz had resigned from teaching to sell automobile insurance. Brick Donovan was expelled and spent weeks in the hospital at Claremont. That summer, he was arrested for assault to be tried as an adult, but plea-bargained down to two years in prison.

Even so, Brick Donovan still received a life sentence. His left leg would never again bend at the knee. Every time he sat, every time he stood, every time he dressed or went to the bathroom, he was reminded of Raymond Reginald Thornton Junior. And he hated him.

Larry Gilmore coughed up blood for two or three days. He spent weeks with his ribs tightly bound, unable to play the drums for the rest of the semester.

Raymond got put on probation, not because he stopped Brick, but as an example to anyone else who might consider fighting at school. Yet it was good to see Brick go. Even the faculty members were relieved. Gradually, Brick faded into a distant memory.

Chapter 15

▼

Leaving It All up to You

Monday, May 6, 1963

It felt strange. Raymond had played "Pomp and Circumstance" at three graduations. But today, Mr. Hooper told him to leave his trombone in the case. It was like saying goodbye to a girl friend.

"Take a break, Thornton. This year you don't get to play." Hooper turned to face the band.

"This has been a splendid year. It's been a lot of fun for me, and we will miss the seniors. We are happy for them. Let's see the hands of those who are graduating."

Out of eighty-two students seventeen raised their hands.

"Let's give them a round of applause."

Never passing up a chance, many of them stood to take a bow. Tony Bergman, first chair flute, stood and curtsied elegantly. He'd do anything for a laugh. He was a stand-up comic until he raised his flute. That was when he went to work. A prodigy with a four-year string of "ones" at contests, he became known statewide for earning a scholarship to Juilliard. But you couldn't tell by watching him on the band bus.

He had a yellow sticker on his flute case that looked like the Yellow Pages logo, except that it said, "Let your fingers do the talking." Tony chose the flute in fifth grade because of its size. He especially relished playing "The Stars and Stripes Forever" because his piccolo was even smaller. The tubas did not find it amusing.

"In fact, each of you seniors must be congratulated," Mr. Hooper said. "Since you are graduating, you can't play at commencement. So, technically, you are no longer band members. That makes you what we call 'backers.' Seniors, prepare to administer 'Hooper's Pledge.'" It was an RHS band tradition. With exaggerated seriousness, he began.

"All the seniors who hold first chair please rise." Nine stood.

"Now, pick up your music folders, and raise your right hand." The seniors were ready.

"Turn to face your replacements. Repeat after me. You have played well and earned the right to be first chair."

"You have played well and earned the right to be first chair."

"Hand over the music."

The seniors did so with extravagant flourishes.

"This sacred honor bears a solemn obligation."

"This sacred honor bears a solemn obligation."

"As first chair of this section ..."

"As first chair of this section ..."

"If you blow a single riff during a performance ..."

"If you blow a single riff during a performance ..."

"I will personally come back ..."

"I will personally come back ..."

"And beat the crap out of you, so help me God."

"And beat the crap out of you, so help me God."

Every year, the pledge generated howls of laughter. But it was not over yet. The students struggled to get serious again. Hooper rapped his baton on the music stand and continued in grave solemnity.

"Now, everyone stand and repeat after me. If I divulge these words outside this room ..."

"*If I divulge these words outside this room …*"
"Or tell another living soul about 'Hooper's Pledge' …"
"*Or tell another living soul about 'Hooper's Pledge' …*"
"Hooper will get fired …"
"*Hooper will get fired …*"
"And I get to carry the kettledrums …"
"*And I get to carry the kettledrums …*"
"In the homecoming parade …"
"*In the homecoming parade …*"
"So help me God."
"*So help me God.*"

Everyone laughed and cheered. Hooper reveled in the moment.

"To laugh is to love," he often said. "And God knows we need the love." Competing band directors wondered why his musicians seldom missed an attack or a cutoff. It was simple. It was the laughter, and it was the love.

He worked the kids hard, so the "pledge" was one of the few times he let them go. When the racket died down, he stepped up on the podium and tapped his baton three times.

"Here we go, folks. Get out 'Pomp and Circumstance.' Seniors, assume your positions." In a thunderous stampede, the seniors grabbed their chairs and stormed off the risers. They formed an intimidating audience.

"Section leaders, this is your moment. Fulfill your oath."

The first run-through was horrific.

"That's okay, folks. That's why we rehearse. 'Hooper's Pledge' only applies to performances. You still have two weeks to live. Let's try again."

It was just what 'Hoop' lived for. He taught them to hear it before they played it and turned them into leaders. When the next run-through improved, the seniors clapped. A couple of them went up on the riser to encourage their sections, kneeling by the music stands to help with the tricky bits. It got better.

It was painful to say good-bye to Mr. Hooper, but the seniors were going on a class trip to Chicago during finals. They all shook Hooper's hand as they filed out. Larry Gilmore was the last one. He received some extra encouragement. Raymond waited for him outside the band room door while the two drummers talked jazz.

"Hey, Larry, there you are. I've been looking for you."

"Man, I know what you mean. We've only had like five classes together today. That really makes it tough," Larry said.

He hooked an arm around Raymond's neck and swung into his arms.

"Now dat you foun' me, Daddy-o, what did you want to axe me?"

Raymond doubled over laughing, collapsing onto the floor with Larry. It was like that play at third base all over again.

"Hey, man, I'm serious," he said after he recovered.

"Uh-oh, dat's bad!"

"C'mon, about the senior trip."

"Yeah, what about it?"

"Three to a room, right?"

"That's what I heard."

"It may be the last chance we get to hang out. How about sharing a room? Whatcha think?"

"It don't mean we're going steady or anything, right?"

"Give me a break."

"Good, 'cause you're not my type."

"Are all drummers crazy?"

"Only the good ones. Look, who'd you have in mind for the third?"

"You have any suggestions?"

"Not offhand. How about Wally or Bud?"

"Wally isn't going. He has to work at the Piggly Wiggly. Bud, maybe."

"Man, we could have a lot of laughs."

"That's what I thought. Let me check with him and get back to you."

"Cool."

"Cool. You be safe."

"You too."

Across the hall, Millie placed her pen on the paper she was grading and lifted her glasses onto the top of her head. She propped her chin on the heel of her hand and thought about what she had just heard. She knew something Raymond didn't. Larry was the only black kid signed up for the trip. And she knew something not even Larry knew. He was the first—ever.

Watching through the classroom window, she studied Raymond as he headed for home. He rode a slow graceful arc up one driveway and back down the next. Effortlessly, he traced a serpentine track between the street and the sidewalk, never missing a drive. It was a metaphor for the way he lived his life. He had a knack for weaving everything together in one continuous motion.

At the bottom of the stairwell, the former first drummer dried his eyes and blew his nose. Then he pushed through the door with a cocky stride and started whistling "Take Five" by Brubeck. *Let's see Hooper get the band to do this,* he thought as he invented a hop-step to suit the 5/4 time. *Paul Desmond blows a cool sax. Joe Morello has a wild set of sticks. And still, these guys are white. Ain't the world full of surprises?*

Chicago

May 13, 1963

Bud knew he was in for trouble, but he agreed anyway. What he didn't expect was to be the bagman of Michigan Avenue. On the train ride to Chicago, Larry and Raymond perfected their rendition of a new release by Dale and Grace called "I'm Leaving It All Up to You." Larry sang Grace, and Raymond took Dale. The original single had a country twang, but when Larry was through, it was 100 percent rock and roll. They were pretty good.

Bud got to stand on the corner with a knitted watch cap and collect money. Chicagoans had an appreciation for raw talent. The boys sang on Michigan Avenue, on the platforms of the El, at the Navy Pier, in front of the NBC Building, and at the Museum of Science and Industry. That was where they had the most fun, and the folks around them could tell.

Next to watching the giant pendulum in the great hall, the best part was singing in the acoustic chamber. Facing into the curved wall, they sang the whole song each time Bud saw someone enter the opposite chamber. It was fun to hear the reaction of people fifty feet away when they suddenly found themselves bathed in falsetto serenade.

> *I'm leavin' it all up to you-ooh-ooh*
> *You decide what you're gonna do*
> *Now do you want my lo-o-ove*
> *Or are we through?*
> *That's why I'm leaving it up to you-ooh-ooh*
> *You decide what you're gonna do*
> *Now do you want my lo-o-ove,*
> *Or are we through*
> *My heart in my hand*
> *I-I don't understand*
> *Baby, what, what have I done wrong*
> *I worship, I worship the ground that you walk on*
> *That's why I'm leavin' it up to you-ooh-ooh*
> *You decide what you're gonna do*
> *Now do you want my lo-o-ove*
> *Or are we through*

Whatever they were expected to do as a large group wasn't nearly as much fun as the stuff they wanted to do together. The boys took advantage of the fact that eleven chaperones had to supervise 120 students. The adults didn't stand a chance. When Mr. Martin asked where they had been all day, they produced their ticket stubs from the museum. How could anyone object to their spending the day at a museum?

Following the ten o'clock bed check, Mr. Martin was burnt out. He would return to the room adjoining theirs, have a couple of beers, and crash. When he started to snore, they were at liberty to resume exploring.

Mostly, they talked—about life, about their futures, and about their ambitions. Two of them were eligible for the draft. Raymond was enrolled at Mizzou to study journalism and had a deferment. Larry was enlisting in the air force to become an aircraft mechanic.

"Music," he said, "was something to fall back on." Raymond was surprised, and Bud was impressed. They enjoyed each other's company even more. It was one of the few times in life when they could talk about their hopes and dreams and about how scary it was to become adults in 1963. They identified their fears and wondered about the purpose of their lives. None of them realized at the time how durable the memories would be from this trip.

Not until Raymond and Bud developed the photos from Chicago did they remember how dark Larry's skin was.

"How could I not notice?" Bud asked.

"It's all in the eyes."

"What?"

"Let's see. How can I explain? When a jazz group really gets going, they don't use music. They just improvise and watch each other's eyes. It's like the music is all in their heads, and they talk with their eyes."

"Can you play without music?"

"Me? No, I'm not that good. But Larry can. He is an improvising fool."

"You telling me that these jazz guys just make it up as they go?"

"Pretty much. Oh, they follow a rough outline, charts, they call it, but it's what comes to them at the moment that they play, not what's written down someplace. Besides, no one knows how to write down some of the stuff these guys play."

"But Mama Rosa used to say that everything is written in the music. I just never learned to read it well enough."

"Bud, stop and think for a minute. Ray Charles can't read music. When he sings, he puts black keys where there aren't any. In 'improv,' no two performances are ever alike. But what really matters is what it says right then—how it feels."

Those balmy days on the shore of Lake Michigan were incredible. And the nights listening to the sets outside the Green Mill on Broadway gave them goose bumps. Sometimes, they could hear the sax crying to the string bass. Other times, the piano poked fun at them from the corners, but the steel brushes on the high-hat stitched it all together. About one thirty one night, some guy named Miles Davis came by with his horn to sit in for awhile. They nearly got caught sneaking back into the hotel.

Years later, Bud realized that he had been watching Larry and Raymond improvise their way through a long, slow good-bye. Take your time. Make it last.

I'm leavin' it all up to you-ooh-ooh
You decide what you're gonna do
Now do you want my lo-o-ove
Or are we through?

Commencement

Sunday, May 26, 1963

"Here we go, now, seniors, act dignified, even if you don't feel like it."

Hooper had done it. The band sounded great. Most bands play "Pomp and Circumstance" with the same enthusiasm as "Ninety-Nine Bottles of Beer on the Wall." Yet, somehow, Raleigh High School's version was regal and energetic, sounding fresh with each repeat.

Larry nodded to him as they lined up in front of their seats. Raymond smiled and waved back thinking, *Uncool, but what the hell?*

"What's the name of that song?" a girl in front of him asked.

"'Pompous Circle Dance,'" Raymond answered.

"What?"

"Never mind."

He wished he could sit with his pals, but diplomas were always handed out in alphabetical order. Students had to line up that way, practically guaranteeing they were surrounded by strangers. Lily Thatcher sat on his right and Bruce Tucker on his left. Lily briefly glanced at him, so Raymond leaned toward her and asked, "Do you come here often?" It took her a moment to realize he was joking.

"Sir, I don't know you. Consequently, I cannot talk to you," she said, keeping a straight face while pretending to be indignant.

Raymond turned to offer his hand to Bruce.

"My name's Thornton, Raymond Thornton. Haven't we met?"

"Maybe. So when do we find out how the Cardinals are doing?"

"Not until this shindig is over, I can tell you. This is the fourth time I have gone through high school graduation, so pardon me for bringing provisions."

That got their attention. He unzipped his robe to retrieve a chocolate bar and his paperback copy of *Catcher in the Rye*. He opened it to page 162 and picked up the story. Things were not going well for Holden Caulfield, and now three seniors were tracking his misadventures. When Raymond noticed them eyeing his candy bar, he sighed, broke it into three parts, and shared it. They might as well make the best of it.

An hour and a half later, it seemed everyone on the dais had made a speech about thresholds. And, of course, not one of them included anything worthy of writing down. As Raymond put it years later, "Theirs was the pomp. Ours was the circumstance." At last, the time came for the graduates to cross the stage. And, of course, it took forever to work their way through the alphabet down to the Ts.

"Raymond Reginald Thornton Junior," the superintendent of schools called out on the PA system as he started across the stage. "Mr. Thornton is the recipient of the 1963 Senior-of-the-Year Award."

The applause swelled, and his pals whistled. No record exists of such an award before or after that date. It never occurred to Raymond to wonder why.

From the back of the auditorium, standing in the shadows under the stairway to the balcony, Brick Donovan glowered in hatred. He never finished high school, and he needed someone to blame.

With a charming smile, Raymond shook hands, claimed his scroll, pulled J. D. Salinger's novel from under his elbow, and put it in the hands of the principal. Then he politely claimed his trophy and strolled away. It seemed to of no more importance than buying a newspaper on the corner.

Seated among her colleagues who were all decked out in their scholastic robes, Millie recognized the book by its cover. She turned away from the audience and bit down on a knuckle to keep from laughing out loud. Tears welled up in her eyes as she trembled with waves of silent laughter.

The majesty of the ceremony collapsed. A flabbergasted Mr. Diener stood center stage, glancing back and forth between the book in his hand and the departing alumnus. A backlog of anxious graduates piled up at the corner of the stage.

Millie had a coughing spell and was forced to study her folded hands for some time before the convulsions stopped. She assured Coach Mertz that she was fine, dabbed at her eyes with a hanky, drew in a large, ragged breath, and pretended to watch the tail end of the procession.

Few had ever found Diener to be a towering intellect. But no one had ever delivered that message quite as effectively. Days later, after his initial fury had dissipated, Diener noticed an inscription on the flyleaf of the book Raymond had placed in his hands.

May 26, 1963
Dear Mr. D.,
I'm leaving it all up to you—
RRT

Chapter 16

▼

The First Wedding

Sunday, June 9, 1963

Darnell and Rosie Milton's living room smelled of flowers, and the furniture had been moved aside for the wedding. Raymond wore a boutonniere on his lapel.

"I presume you know I don't approve of this," Mr. Grayson said.

"Uncle Bill, please. Not here. You wanna talk, we can go outside."

The front porch was freshly painted. Raymond walked out to the wide railing and sat down. The future father-in-law slumped down in the swing. Raymond couldn't help thinking that Uncle Bill's comb-over was a bad idea. It would be better to just go bald.

"Tell me what's bugging you, Mr. G.?"

"You probably figured out I don't like this whole shotgun wedding business. By the time Wally graduates, his girlfriend has a bun in the oven, so he has to get married and go to work at the Piggly Wiggly to support her."

"Whoa. Wait. I'm with you up to a point, but don't forget Betty is a bright girl, not some empty-headed princess. She is head over heels in love with Wally, and he'll do anything for her. I believe they can make it work."

"I should have known you'd stick up for him."

"Aw, c'mon, Uncle Bill, I'm trying to stick up for Betty. She's a prize."

"But, Raymond, fathers look at things differently. It's like Wally's whole future got hijacked by one night of passion. I'm not sure he can go from being a kid to being a dad just like that," he said, snapping his fingers.

While Raymond thought about this, Mr. Grayson kneaded his hands, his eyes darting around like those of a man looking for an exit.

"Mr. G., it's natural for you to worry about them. But that doesn't mean your worst fears are going to come true."

"Oh yeah? What do you know about it?"

An awkward silence hung in the air between them. Raymond leaned in toward him until they made eye contact.

"You know all those years you coached us in Little League?"

"How could I forget?"

"The most important thing you ever taught us had nothing to do with hitting or running or throwing."

"What are you telling me, I missed the fundamentals?"

"No, I'm serious. It stuck with me all this time. You told us once that a champion is the guy who not only does his job, but also helps his teammates do theirs."

"Yeah, well, I said a lot of things back then—Most of it, I don't recall."

"Yeah, well, some of us do."

After a moment, Raymond spoke. "Do you mind if I ask you a personal question?"

"It's okay, I guess."

"You and Dad went to school together, right?"

"Yeah, we did."

"Did you go to Mom and Dad's wedding?"

"That was a long time ago."

"I know, but do you remember anything about it? Were you there when Mom and Dad got married?"

"No, I ... I don't think I was there."

"Well, I was."

Uncle Bill's mouth dropped open, but no words came out.

"That's when Dad went to work at the tire store. Now, he owns it. He's happy."

"Raymond, I didn't know. I apologize."

"It's okay. See, eighteen years later, it doesn't matter."

Bill Grayson sat with his hands braced against his knees. Raymond rose and started for the door. He paused long enough to place a hand on the man's shoulder.

"So tell me, Uncle Bill, you gonna spoil that grandkid?" and he was gone.

Mr. Grayson stared at his shoes for awhile and then buried his face in his hands. He fished out his handkerchief and blew his nose. After a minute or so, he grunted and stood.

Okay, Big Bill, he thought as he put the handkerchief away, *go in there, and do your job.*

Hearing him pull the door closed behind him, Miss Millie took a moment to regain her composure. Then she stepped around the corner of the house and carried a bowl of fruit salad across the porch.

When the last folding chair was set up, Uncle Bill went over to Raymond and put an arm around his shoulders.

"Thanks," he said.

"Don't mention it, Coach."

Villanova

Friday, June 21, 1963

The ball glanced off the outfielder's glove and hopped into tall grass. Bud rounded to second. The pain in his foot warned him against trying for third. He hadn't sprinted this hard since Poncho tried to rip off his toes. Knowing that Wally was batting next, he was glad he got to second. It gave him a lead on his lanky teammate. Otherwise, Wally would run him down somewhere short of home plate. While the pitcher and batter studied each other, he tagged up and sidestepped toward third, trying to stay loose and catch his breath.

Bud ran flat-out today instead of favoring his foot. It was partly due to his news and partly to the smell of newly cut grass on a June afternoon. He wanted to enjoy himself as much as possible before he left town.

"Last" Presbyterian had been handed a miracle. They were two runs up on Living Word Lutheran. Their game was haphazard due to erratic practice. Not so for the Lutherans, they were a machine. Of all the things they took seriously, the church league topped the list. Since defeat at the hands of Presbyterians would mean a year of humiliation, they did what any good Lutheran would do. They bore down.

The Catholics in the bleachers cheered both teams on because they played the winner. An exhausted champion was easier to defeat. On the other hand, their frequent trips to the kegs balanced the odds. It was a sporting way to go at it.

Meanwhile, receipts in the concession stand exceeded Baptist expectations. Not yet three o'clock, they were already stuffing bags of cash behind the seat in Brother Whittaker's pickup.

The Baptists had it figured out. Let the proud and the haughty contend against one another in the name of God. It wouldn't change a thing since they were all bound for perdition anyway. Meanwhile, the Baptists needed to pay for the new fellowship hall.

Somebody noticed they were almost out of miniature paddles to go with each tub of ice cream. The committee chairman called for his swiftest runner. She was all legs and ran like a deer.

"Bring us more spoons, even if you have to buy plastic!"

The little girl's pigtails flew out behind her as she picked up speed, a five-dollar bill clutched in her hand.

"Can you guess which event is my favorite?" Betty Ann Grayson asked. She slipped a hand under Wally's arm and looked up at him as they strolled along. She was tall and willowy, with a strong jaw, a keen intellect, auburn hair, and laughing hazel eyes that missed nothing. Having grown up with four brothers, even when she "dressed up like a girl," she was at home in the company of rowdies.

"Let me think about that for a moment," Wally said.

Her eyes sparkled with mischief as she waited.

"I'd say it has to be the reading of the winning essay."

"Nope." She turned to walk backwards, trusting Wally to steer her clear of obstacles.

"Raymond, what's your guess?" she asked.

"Well, it can't be the ball game, because we always lose." He was still brooding about the Lutherans.

"That's a statement, not a guess. Come on, take a guess."

"Well, the music is usually pretty good—barbershop, banjos, guitars, big band tunes. Is that it?"

"Nope. Bud, what do you think?"

He stopped to consider.

"Well, Betty, let's see." He used his fingers to tick of the choices. "If it's not the ball game, and if it's not the entertainment, and if it's not the reading, that only leaves one thing."

"What?"

"The homemade ice cream."

"Hmmmm. I forgot about that. Now I have to revise my list. Okay, what I really meant is what do you think my *second* most favorite thing is?"

The boys tried to guess. Pony rides? Nope. Writing workshops? Nope. Melodramas? Nope. They each gave up.

"It's the Liars Club."

"Of course," Wally said. "That makes perfect sense."

"You should have known," said Bud. "You're her husband. You're supposed to know stuff like that."

Wally turned and pointed at him.

"You're the detective. You should have figured it out."

"Me? Don't point at me. Besides, it's all Raymond's fault."

"My fault? How do you figure that?"

"Umm, let's see. Okay. Here we go. Instead of answering Betty's question, you made a statement, but it eliminated a possibility. That means it was the same thing as sneaking in an extra guess. That got me to wondering whether you were actually clever or just a cheater. So I was distracted all because of you. There. See, it's really very simple."

"Liar."

"Cheat."

"But very impressive."

"Thank you."

"A lie, but very impressive."

"Thank you. I try."

They bought chips and barbecue from the Kiwanis Club, fetching bottles of Royal Crown out of an ice-filled tub, and went over to sit in the shade on the steps of the courthouse. It was more than a half hour before the storytelling began, but it was the best way to get a seat in the grass. In fact, the courthouse lawn was filling up with blankets and folding lawn chairs.

Originally intended to showcase oral narrative, the "Storytelling Contest" rapidly devolved into "The Liars Club." Raleigh Countians preferred hilarity over eloquence any day. After all, bragging rights were involved.

Concessionaires knew a good thing when they saw it and provided a public address system and footlights. Then they put spotlights on the roof of the bank. One night a year, the courthouse steps became a stage.

"I've got something I want to tell you guys," Bud said.

That was when he told them about Villanova.

At the end of the program, there was a stampede for ice cream. The entrepreneurs took note of the size of the crowd and pulled out their ice buckets to crank out emergency supplies. At fifty cents a bowl, there was money to be made.

"Bud, I'm happy for you," Betty Ann said, spooning out her next bite. "But I didn't know you were going to college. I thought you wanted to go into police work."

"I do, but not just cop stuff. I want to study forensics and learn how to take fingerprints, find evidence, to use science to get crooks off the streets. You know I love a mystery, so why not make it a career?"

Bud glanced at Wally and Raymond. His pals understood where this came from, and they knew where it would lead.

"Okay, good," said Wally, trying to swallow a spoonful of ice cream without getting a brain-freeze. "So why Villanova? Doesn't that take like four years or something? That's gotta cost a lotta dough."

"I don't have that much," Bud answered. "I only have enough for about two years, and that's really stretching it."

"Then you've got some serious explaining to do, partner."

"Look, here's how it works. Most of the time, guys learn this stuff by going through some sort of police academy. With my bum foot, I can't get in. So what's the alternative? Community college? It's cheap, but you compete with all your classmates when you apply for a job. I need something that will set me apart."

"So how does Villanova do that?" Raymond asked.

"Their criminal justice program is famous. Police chiefs and wardens and guys like that go there to study. Now let's say you want to hire a new guy to work crime scenes. You have one applicant with an associate degree from Podunk Community College. Another guy has two years at Villanova. Which one are you going to want to look at?"

"Smart," Wally said, pointing at him with his spoon. "That's very smart."

"In two years, I can finish all the courses for a minor in criminal justice, and that should carry some clout."

"I don't understand about minors and majors. Explain," Betty said.

"I'm not an expert, but let's say I go to Villanova for four years and major in business management. If I complete the right CJ courses, I can graduate with a major in business and a minor in criminal justice. I figure it's my ace in the hole to show that in two years, I knocked down the requirements for a minor in CJ at Villanova."

"You're not going for a degree. You're going for an interview!" Wally blurted out, nearly dumping his bowl of ice cream on the ground.

"Bingo!"

"And you call me a cheat!" Raymond laughed. "I knew there was a scheme. You always have one. So how are you gonna pay for all this?"

"Dad left me a little college money in a life insurance policy. Mom didn't tell me until last Christmas. It's not enough for four years, but it's enough to get me started. The rest is up to me."

"Wow. I am impressed," Raymond said. "Not bad for a liar."

"And a cheat."

"You take the prize, man. You take the prize." Raymond reached over to shake his hand. Wally slugged Bud on the shoulder.

"Way to go," said Betty. "And Wally said you would never amount to anything. Of course, I never believed him. Way to go."

They congratulated Bud and speculated about his future. That night, they believed they would be friends for life. Brick Donovan watched and waited.

Chapter 17

▼

The Fourth Estate

Friday, November 22, 1963

Raymond would remember standing in the stairwell of Loeb Hall for the rest of his life. He was on the third step from the bottom, waiting in line for lunch.

"Hey, have you heard? Somebody shot the president."

"I don't know what the punch line is," Raymond replied, "but that's not funny."

"No, no! It's no joke. I'm serious, man. I just heard on the radio a couple of minutes ago that Kennedy got shot in Dallas."

"He's okay, though, right?"

"I don't know. He was shot in the head. They rushed him to a hospital. He could die." A helpless shrug told everyone it was true.

Three words pulled reality inside out: *He could die.* Soon, reliable sources would tell the world it was true.

TV journalists of that day, men like Edward R. Murrow, Walter Cronkite, Chet Huntley, and David Brinkley, had earned the public trust. Through their eyes and words, a nation bore witness to the murder of one president, the swearing-in of another in front of a widow in a bloodied dress, the televised killing of Lee Harvey Oswald, and the solemnity of a state funeral. Thanksgiving 1963 was the most somber national holiday in living memory.

Journalism in those days was the "make-a-difference-with-the-truth" kind. What Raymond had not yet learned is that truth is seldom simple or obvious. But all that would change at Anh Khe. Meanwhile, the events of his college years electrified every serious journalist into recognizing the public trust.

The year 1963 was the newsman's year. The 114-day-old newspaper strike in New York City ended on April Fool's Day. Segregationists, including Alabama Governor George Wallace, were unable to suppress the Civil Rights movement in Birmingham. To their way of thinking, Negro civil disobedience made white folks look bad. But in the end, it was the bombing death of four teenage girls and Police Commissioner "Bull" Connors who did it. He ordered the police and fire departments to turn the dogs and fire cannons loose on children. Because of him, President Kennedy and the rest of the world saw bigotry at its worst.

In June, Valentina Vladimirovna Tereshkova was the first woman launched into space, and Medgar Evers, a civil rights leader and D-Day survivor, was shot in the back in Mississippi. He had already experienced a firebombing at his home and an attempt to run him down with a car. He died in front of his home just hours after Kennedy delivered a televised speech affirming civil rights.

On August 28, a quarter of a million black Americans rallied in the nation's capitol to hear Dr. Martin Luther King Jr. declare, "I have a dream..." On October 28, the Cuban Missile Crisis ended. Twenty-five days later, a sniper shot John F. Kennedy in the head at Dealey Plaza. Forty-eight hours and seven minutes later, Jack Ruby stepped in front of police to shoot Lee Harvey Oswald in the side.

By 1964, Raymond viewed the world through the eyes of a journalist. He penned an article in the *Columbia Missourian* about Dr. Martin Luther King Jr. winning the Nobel Peace Prize. Four years later, this leader too would die at the hands of a rifleman, this time in Memphis.

In 1964, Jimmy Hoffa was convicted of jury-rigging, the Warren Commission claimed Lee Harvey Oswald acted alone, Lyndon B. Johnson won by a landslide, the Soviet Union launched spy satellites, and Jack Ruby was sentenced to die for killing Oswald.

In 1965, President Johnson authorized U.S. forces to fight in Vietnam and sent an additional 50,000 troops, yet stopped the bombing to offer peace. Martin Luther King Jr. led the Alabama Freedom Walk. Malcolm X, the spokesman for the Nation of Islam, was assassinated in Harlem, and 25,000 marched on Washington to protest the Vietnam War.

In 1966, a mid-air collision between a B-52 and a KC-135 tanker killed seven airmen and scattered four nuclear weapons across the countryside near Palomares, Spain. Three struck land, and one plunged into the Mediterranean, to be recovered months later. Of those striking land, high explosives detonated in two, scattering radioactive material across the Spanish countryside.

Russia landed on the moon. Three astronauts died in an Apollo mission test, and James Meredith, the first black student at the University of Mississippi, was shot during a civil rights march. He survived. The photo of him writhing on the sidewalk won the 1967 Pulitzer Prize for Jack R. Thornell.

In 1967, troop strength in Vietnam reached 525,000. One of them was Raymond Reginald Thornton Jr., age 21, a newspaper reporter from Raleigh. For reasons of his own, he put his journalism career on hold and enlisted in the army. It was as simple as this: He could still hear John F. Kennedy saying, "Ask not what your country can do for you. Ask what you can do for your country."

Raymond knew the quote. It didn't stop there. Kennedy went on to say, "My fellow citizens of the world, ask not what America will do for you, but what together we can do for the freedom of man."

Chapter 18

▼

Coming Home

Thursday, November 13, 1969

Raymond rode into town with all his worldly goods strapped to a dusty FLH Electra-Glide. Aside from what he wore, he owned two pairs of jeans, a handful of tee shirts, a useless dress uniform, a model M1911A1 .45, and a bottle of J&B Scotch. The handgun was a war trophy. He kept it in honor of some unknown GI who first carried it into battle. The Scotch was to help him forget the PAVN officer he killed in a tunnel to get it back. Otherwise, he would have to change the sheets every night.

The America he remembered was gone. Five months earlier, the army had spat him back out into the world from Ft. Lewis, Washington. The government's last gift to him was a stack of travel requests to get him back to his home of record. To use them, he had to be in uniform. Hippies at Sea-Tac Airport spat on him and accused him of butchering babies. Raymond decided he was going to have to kill them. They saw it in his eyes and fled, leaving behind only the coppery scent of fear in the air.

The nurse at Ft. Lewis had been right. He had death in his eyes. Having no compelling reason to go to St. Louis, he tore up the TRs and left the airport.

"Where to, soldier?" the cabbie asked, opening the trunk for the duffle bag.

"Just get me away from here. Is there a J. C. Penney's nearby?"

"There's one at Southcenter. That where you wanna go?"

"That'll do."

The driver shrugged, tossed in the duffle, and slammed the trunk lid closed. Raymond jumped at the sound and dove for cover. Only moments later, the cabbie slammed the driver's door behind him, and Raymond hit the floor.

The astonished cabbie watched in the rearview mirror as his fare crawled back into the seat. He pulled away from the curb in silence. A lot of GIs he saw were edgy like that. Some slept. Some talked. This one stared out the window. The driver decided not to make any more sudden moves or loud noises.

Raymond down-shifted the Harley and pulled into the Phillips 66 station, ringing the bell twice as he rolled across the pneumatic hose. He killed the engine and, bracing the bike with his legs, closed his eyes to remember the sound of that bell from an earlier lifetime.

In one fluid motion, he propped the bike on its kickstand and swept his right leg high over the duffle bag behind him to stand. It was a dance move he practiced daily. It made a teenage kid drinking a Coca-Cola in the shade envious.

The gas station attendant came out wiping his greasy hands with a filthy shop rag.

"Hand-crank-on-the-left-clears-the-meter. Lift-the-nozzle-to-start-the-pump. Let-me-know-if-you-need-anything-else. Pay-me-when-you're-done."

"Where's Gil?"

"Who?"

"Goofy Gil, the Gas Guy."

"There are lots of goofy guys around here, but nobody named Gil." The attendant ducked back inside.

Raymond squeezed four-point-three gallons into the Harley and handed the guy two dollar bills and accepted his change without a word. He mounted with a smooth, high swing of the right leg, folded the kickstand up with a kick from his left heel, thumbed the starter, and pulled out of the lot heading toward Main Street. Rumbling down the cobblestone boulevard, he wondered if this was the place he and his buddies had been fighting and dying for. But no one here seemed to care. To the folks on the streets of Raleigh, he was just another suspicious guy with a ragged beard on a motorcycle. The last day he had shaved was the day he got out of the army.

Still filthy from the jungle, he had gotten off the 747 at McChord Air Force Base and reclaimed his duffle and his guns. Buses hauled everyone over to the armory to check their weapons. Then they were trucked off to the showers to flush away the stench of Vietnam. Raymond cleaned up, donned a new set of khakis complete with nametag, insignia, and medals, and went back to the armory to claim his guns.

"Sir, how may I help you?" Sergeant Moody asked from behind the counter.

"Lieutenant Thornton, here to claim my weapons."

"Okay, sir. How long ago did you check them in?"

"Just this morning, Sergeant. In fact, I gave them to you. An AK-47 and a .45. I'm outta here. I'm going home."

"We haven't filed this morning's paperwork yet, so let me go look in the in-box."

Moody stepped over to a wire basket full of inventory cards and started riffling through them. Raymond followed him down the counter, watching for his handwriting. After a tedious search, Sergeant Moody pulled out two cards.

"Aha!" he said. "Here we go. Model 1911A1. Aisle 7, rack 62C, inventory control number 7006562. Be right back, sir."

He unlocked the cage and disappeared behind the steel shelving. A couple minutes later, he returned with a .45. He racked the slide open so they could both see there was no round chambered and laid it on the rubber countertop. Comparing the numbers on the card to the tag on the trigger guard and serial number on the frame, he initialed the card and spun it around for Raymond to sign. Raymond cross-checked the numbers and signed for the gun.

"Okay. Now let's get the AK."

Sergeant Moody looked at the second card.

"AK-47. Aisle 12, rack 29e, ICN 7006563. Okay, sir. Hold on."

Moody didn't come back.

"Sergeant Adelson?" Moody called from a great distance. "Can you come here for a second? I can't find this gun."

A staff sergeant let himself through the cage door and headed back toward Moody's voice.

"What're you looking for?"

"That AK-47 that came in this morning."

"Aw, shit. I was afraid of that."

Raymond got a familiar queasy feeling in the pit of his stomach and knew things had just taken a turn for the worse. He vaulted the counter and waited.

Moody started making excuses even before he got to the cage door.

"I don't know what to tell you, Lieutenant, but there ain't no AK-47 back there. I searched everywhere ..."

The cage door struck him in the face, shattering his nose and splitting his forehead. Raymond grabbed him by the shirt and belt buckle and threw him over the counter. By the time he hit the floor, Raymond was on top of him. He rolled him over onto his back, pinned his arms under his knees, and grabbed him by both ears.

"What ... do ... you ... mean," he screamed, pounding Moody's head against the floor with each word, "you ... don't ... know ... where ... it ... is?"

Spittle flew from his mouth. Moody was finished. Raymond heard the sound of running footsteps heading his way. He jumped to his feet, grabbed the .45 with his left hand, tucked it out of sight under his right arm, crossed his legs, and leaned nonchalantly on the counter on his elbows.

Adelson hit the cage door at a full sprint and skidded to a stop when he saw a lieutenant leaning on the counter casually.

"What the hell is going on …?"

"Well, Sarge, it looks like some of your boys stole my AK-47."

"Don't be absurd. That doesn't happen here … Jesus Christ! What happened to Moody?"

"The same thing that's about to happen to you."

Adelson's face purpled with rage, but he never saw it coming. All he got out was, "Why, you …"

Raymond's backhand struck like a snake. Two pounds of gun-metal collided with the side of Adelson's head. He dropped like a stone. Raymond grabbed him by the collar and dragged him out into the middle of the floor, dumping him next to Moody. Then he went behind the counter, slammed the cage door closed, and picked up the phone. By the time everyone else in the section rushed in, he was in the middle of a phone call.

"Military police? Yeah, this is Lieutenant Raymond R. Thornton Jr. I'm at the armory where I signed in an AK-47 this morning, and the damned thing has already been stolen. I just knocked the living shit out of two NCOs who lied to me about it, and right now, I'm looking at ten or twelve guys who really don't want to piss me off. Maybe you should send someone over. I'm at extension … extension …"

He looked around until someone told him.

"Extension 4412."

He hung up the phone.

"All right, gentlemen. Maybe you noticed … a year and a half in the jungle has strained my sense of humor. So which one of you sons of bitches wants to fuck with me next?"

They stood around him and waited. He was, after all, the ranking man in the room.

Four MPs showed up with weapons drawn. When they walked in on the standoff, Raymond raised two empty hands. They stowed their weapons and took over. Master Sergeant Jacoby, the NCO in charge of the detail, made his way through the crowd to speak to Raymond, stepping over two unconscious men on the floor. He touched the lieutenant's elbow gingerly to turn him away from the crowd so they could talk.

"You want to tell me just exactly what the hell is going on here, sir?"

He asked questions and listened intently to Raymond's answers. Not even the men close to them could overhear. It went on for several minutes. When Jacoby had heard enough, he turned around to the others.

"All right, you assholes, listen up," he said in a booming voice. "The lieutenant here started out a buck private two years ago just like the rest of us at Fort Leonard Wood, went to war as a combat engineer, and ended up a door gunner with the Air Cav."

He pointed to Raymond's colors.

"Two Purple Hearts, a Bronze Star, a Silver Star, Valor under Fire—this ain't doodads out of a box of Crackerjacks, gentlemen. And this ain't no ROTC butter-bar. This here's a genuine Mustang, battlefield commission. What you got here is a warrior. So get your shit straight. Where the hell's his AK-47?"

The two bleeding NCOs were pulled off the floor and mopped up enough to document the "mysterious disappearance" of Raymond's weapon. Then an ambulance came to haul them off to Madigan Army Medical Center. After all, the LT had done it right. He had registered a confiscated weapon and left it in the armory for safekeeping. Now it was gone. When the paperwork was finished, Master Sergeant Jacoby handed a copy to Raymond.

"Sorry, sir. I have to take you in. There's still the matter of the assault. Someone above my pay grade will have to sort it out."

"I understand," Raymond said, holding his wrists out for cuffs.

"That won't be necessary, sir. Will it?"

"No."

Jacoby gestured for Raymond to lead the way.

Someone in the room called, "Ten-hut." With the exception of four MPs and two bleeding NCOs, every soldier in the room snapped to attention. Raymond turned to acknowledge them and said, "Thank you, gentlemen," and then stepped through the door. Once in the car, Master Sergeant Jacoby turned to look at him wedged in the back seat between two MPs.

"Lieutenant, sir?"

"Yeah?"

"About your AK-47. Sir, I'm pretty sure it's gone. All kinds of things vanish out the back door of this place, and we can't seem to stop it."

Raymond sighed and rubbed his face with both hands.

"I know, Sarge. That whole thing back there wasn't just about an AK, anyway. It was about the grunts bleeding and dying in Nam while these jackasses sit around falsifying records and stealing guns."

"With all due respect, sir, you get to stop fighting the war and go home. I suggest you not screw it up."

"Sounds like a plan."

"Sir, let me see if I got my chronology right," Jacoby said twisting further around in the front seat. "As soon as you found out the gun had gone missing, you called the MPs, right?"

"What?"

"That's what he said, isn't it?" Jacoby asked the driver.

"That's what I heard him say, Sergeant," the driver answered.

Jacoby looked at the two MPs in the back seat and said, "Well?"

The one on Raymond's left shrugged. The other said, "That's how I remember it."

"And those two baboons back there jumped you while you were making the call, right?" Jacoby said, looking at Raymond.

"Well, that's not exactly …"

"They assaulted a superior officer, and you were forced to defend yourself? Is that about right, sir? You know, I want my report to be accurate."

"Look, you don't have to do this, you know."

"Sir, when a soldier gets a battlefield commission in his first hitch, you can bet he saved some asses besides his own. I don't figure that AK-47 was a birthday present, so let me do my part now. Go home. Chase girls. Start living again. You're entitled."

"You been over?"

"Naw. I just seen what it does to the guys coming back. By now, I can tell the difference between tunnel rats and office wienies."

"How so?"

"Neither one much gives a shit what I think. But the guy who goes down a hole after Charlie figuring he's going to die down there don't have to tell you. It just shows. It's a look he gets."

"A nurse called it 'killer eyes.'"

"Sir, I don't know what to call it, but you got it. Those guys back there are gonna have a hard time forgetting this day. You prob'ly did more to stop bootlegging in five minutes than we could have done with a dozen court martials. Ass-whuppins like that one get personal."

Without thinking, Raymond turned left to pass in front of the courthouse and waited at Raleigh's only stoplight. When it turned green, he idled across Business 19 and down the hill towards the *Journal-Messenger* office. There, he propped his bike on the kickstand across from a group of paperboys. He dismounted and rested his butt against the seat, his long legs crossed and stretching out into the street. The boys were telling lies while folding papers and glancing at the unnerving stranger drinking Scotch right out of the bottle. They hurried to get on their way, trying not to glance over their shoulders as they pumped up the hill toward town.

I wonder if Lou Baxter would be willing to hire me again, he thought. *Probably not while I'm half drunk and looking like hammered shit.* He took another long pull on the bottle of J&B and decided he was drunk enough to go see Thornton Tire and Auto. His dad had died at the shop while Raymond was calling in artillery on the perimeter at Camp Radcliff.

He was climbing the ladder to the tower just before midnight when VC and PAVN regulars started blowing tripwires out on the line and claymores started going off. Up in the tower was an E-8 who was three-quarters drunk. Raymond figured he'd fall off the ladder and break his neck so he told him just to sit down—he would look out for him. It was the beginning of the Tet Offensive.

Raymond called in artillery and gunships and tried to repel the intruders with his M-16 until it overheated and jammed. The spare barrel was useless when you needed it. The jammed barrel was always too hot to change out. That was when he moved to the M60 machine gun to hold back the wave of humanity trying to cross the 100-yard perimeter. The lights were on; flares were in the sky. It was insanity, yet the wave kept coming across the barren earth and dying.

Hours later, after the assault had been turned back, a captain came up from the Air Cav to talk to the team who called in the artillery and manned the machine gun. When he got up there, he found one combat engineer and a master sergeant passed out drunk. Amazed, he told Raymond, "You come with me." The night his dad died was the night Raymond earned his Bronze Star.

His mother fell apart. Despondent, she couldn't even keep her job at J. C. Penney's. She left Raleigh to go live with her sister in Milwaukee. Between what they could get for the inventory and tools at the shop and what the house and furniture sold for, it almost got her out of debt.

Raymond rolled up on the weedy ramp in front and studied the shell of what had once been a fortress of safety in his life. The front wall was covered with graffiti. The windows were broken, and a weathered "For Sale or Lease" sign hung crookedly inside the shattered office door. It reminded him of so many shelled-out bunkers he had seen. He shut down the bike, fell while dismounting, and crawled over to the saddlebag to pull the bottle out.

When he finished it, he threw it through the front window and passed out. He came to in the county jail, the cell door standing wide open, with a silent figure sitting in the shadows across from him on the opposite bunk.

"How's your head, Raymond?"

"Oh, jeez, it's not real good right now. It feels like it's been used for batting practice."

"You got a pretty good cut above your eye. Looks like you split it open when you fell. I cleaned it up and put a butterfly on it. If that doesn't work, you may need stitches."

"Ouch, oh, man. I see what you mean. Where am I? How did I get here? Who are you?"

"You're in the Raleigh County jail. The city cops brought you in after someone reported a dead body in front of your dad's old shop. It's Bud, Bud Oswald, Deputy Oswald to you, given your apparent state of public intoxication. Neighbors said they heard glass breaking and saw a body. Since the old place belongs to you anyhow, they can't charge you with destroying someone else's property."

"Bud. I was going to come looking for you, but I didn't get that far. Am I under arrest?"

"No."

"Why not?"

"Beats the hell out of me. You got any place to stay?"

"No, I was going to find you or Wally to see if there was a place to crash."

"Well, you found me, and you have these accommodations for tonight. Sleep it off, and we'll see if you can make any sense in the daylight," Bud said, rising to leave.

"Hey, Bud?"

"Yeah?"

"Do me a favor, will ya?"

"What's that?"

"Lock the cell door when you leave."

"Why?"

"Two reasons: one, to keep me in; and two, to keep Charlie out. I haven't been able to sleep since Nam."

"What do you mean?"

"The flight into Da Nang was like fifteen or sixteen hours. Twenty of us were put in a tent to get some sleep. We'd been in Nam about two hours when somebody tossed a grenade in through an open flap. Killed half the combat engineers in my unit. I was the furthest away. Sometimes at night, I can still smell it, hear it, and taste it. I haven't had a decent night's sleep since. I would just feel safer with the cell door locked."

"God almighty, Ray. All right. I'll keep the bad guys out for tonight. But you're going to have to work something else out for tomorrow. When you wake up in the morning, I'll get some coffee inside you, and we'll go get your bike."

There was no answer. Bud heard the sound of ragged breathing, slid the cell door closed with a clank, and left. He left shaking his head, thinking, *Raymond may be home, but he is still not with us.*

Chapter 19

The VA Hospital

Friday, January 2, 1970

Three figures appeared on Millie's porch in the middle of the night. Two men were practically carrying a third. Bud took off his hat and rang the bell. He was surprised to see lights on in the back hall and even more surprised to see somebody answering the door promptly at this hour.

"Who is it?" Millie asked through the locked door.

"Bud and Wally. We need to put Raymond in his room."

"Is he drunk?"

"Yes, ma'am, he is."

"Give me a moment."

She opened the door. She wore a blue bathrobe, her red hair falling to her waist.

"No more. You can't keep bringing him here anymore. Tomorrow, I will take all his stuff out of his room and leave it on the porch. When he gets out of jail, tell him to come get it. I'll give him back January's rent, but I've had it. No more."

"Yes, ma'am."

She left the porch light on but closed the door.

"Betty says the same thing," Wally said. "He scares the kids, and she never knows what he will say or do. So what now, Bud?"

"This time, he goes into detox. He can stay there until somebody gets his attention for all I care."

"It ain't gonna be pretty, is it?"

"No, I'm fairly sure it is not. But something's got to give. I've even talked to the VA hospitals. I think we're on our own here. So let's get him in the car. We have to haul him over to Claremont."

Miss Millie was true to her word. At daybreak, all of Raymond's possessions were on the porch in paper bags from the Piggly Wiggly. They stayed there for four days. When Raymond showed up to collect them, he was pale and shaky, but he was sober.

"Miss Millie, I apologize for what I put you through. I have these terrible nightmares, so I drink to keep from dreaming."

"Raymond, I have known you for a long time. I cannot imagine what you saw in Vietnam, but I will not be a party to your self-destruction. You were a writer once. Are you going to kill that too? Do something about it. Get help. Get medicine. But you will not commit extended suicide, one sip at a time, while you are living here."

"I'm going to the VA to get some help. If I can get straightened out, can I come back? I really don't have any place else to go."

"I'm not making promises. If you come back and I have rented out the room, the answer is no. If you come back the way you have been these past months, the answer is no. If you come back truly changed and serious about holding a job, the answer is maybe. We'll just have to see."

"Maybe is good. It's more than I deserve. I don't want to disappoint you or anyone else. I just can't get the images out of my head."

"Raymond, there has to be a way. Talk them out. Write them out. What's killing you is keeping them inside. You can't handle that. Either write them down or die. Do it for yourself and the guys who went over there with you—those who came back and those who didn't."

Raymond's eyes closed briefly, and he turned to look toward the hedge along the sidewalk. Tears flowed down his cheeks. His shoulders quaked from the effort to avoid breaking down. He turned to face her with clenched jaws, struggling to maintain his composure. When at last he could speak, it was in a whisper.

"There are others. I had two buddies who made it back with me. We traveled together back to their homes. We bought bikes in Seattle and rode to Indiana. They are both dead now. The week after I left, Mackey went out to the barn with a shotgun and killed himself. Not long after, Rogers ... I heard he closed himself up in his garage, started the engine, and died in the front seat of his car."

"My God, Raymond! And you have been working on killing yourself with the Scotch. You've got to get help."

He sank to the porch steps and buried his face in his hands, sobbing like a child. Millie crossed to the steps, sat next to him, leaned against him, and placed an arm around his shoulders.

"Look, I care too much about you to watch you go over the edge without a fight. You were always special to me, Wally and Bud too, but you most of all. Please, Raymond! You owe it to Mackey and Rogers. Tell their stories. Don't let them survive the war just to die at home for nothing. You are a journalist. So prove it!"

Thursday, January 8, 1970
First Presbyterian Church

The time had come in history for women to be ordained as elders in the Presbyterian Church. Margaret Millicent McKenna was the first in the Central Highlands Presbytery. At 9:38 PM, the doors opened from the fellowship hall to the parking lot. Yellow light spilled out onto the stoop as the members of the finance committee pulled on hats, gloves, and scarves and stepped out into the falling snow. Lou Baxter, ever the gentleman, escorted Millie to her '62 Buick Special.

"It's a shame about Vernie. What do you think Clarence will do now that she's gone?" asked Millie.

"We talked about that after the funeral. He told me he was thinking about selling the place and setting up a woodworking shop somewhere in town. Said he was getting too old to farm and that most of his income came from construction jobs anyway."

"Tell him that I have a room for rent if he needs one."

"Okay, I'll do that."

Lou retrieved a snow scraper from his '68 Karmann Ghia and returned to help her clean her windshield.

"I thought you rented your room to Ray Thornton."

"I did. But I threw him out."

Lou stood upright, shoved his glasses back up on his nose, and said, "What?"

"That's right. He went off to war the all-American boy and came home the all-American drunk. I need the money, but not enough to get up all hours of the night so that Bud and Wally can haul him upstairs to bed. He's gone. I'll take a heartbroken old man over a half-crazy Vietnam Vet any day."

"Millie, those are pretty harsh words coming from you. I'm surprised. I always thought he was one of your favorites."

She stopped scraping and stared off into the distance. She sniffed and wiped her eyes with the cuff of her sleeve.

"That's what makes it so hard, Lou. He is. But sleep deprivation takes its toll. The nights he isn't out carousing, he wakes me up with nightmares. I hear him yelling and bumping around. One night, he crept down the stairs with a gun in his hand. After he figured out where he was, he sat on the porch swing until dawn. He scares me to death."

Now it was Lou's turn to be silent.

"What's the matter, Lou? … Lou? Are you all right?"

Lou turned slowly toward her, removed his hat with one hand, and wiped his forehead. Then he put the hat back on with both hands.

"He came to me looking for a job. Something about it didn't feel right, so I told him I would have to think about it and look at the financials. So what do we do, Millie?"

"I don't know," she said, opening the door and rolling the window down. She slid in behind the steering wheel and closed the door. Lou waited. She started the engine and leaned out the window to finish her answer. "I don't know what you're going to do, but I'm going to do the only thing I can."

"What's that?"

"Pray. Just like I have been since the day he came home. And I plan to keep on doing it until something changes. Good night, Lou. Thanks for cleaning my windows."

"G'night, Millie."

She rolled up the window and drove off. Lou stood there in the falling snow studying her tire tracks for a long time. Then he cleaned off the VW and went home to his family.

Chapter 20

The Tenant

Tuesday, March 17, 1970

Raymond had just finished brewing coffee over the camp stove in bay number two when a pickup truck pulled into the parking lot. The driver's door creaked open, and an old man in coveralls got out and slammed it shut. He headed towards the boarded office. He shoved the door open slightly and jingled the bells hanging on the push bar, calling inside through the crack.

"Hello? Anybody here?"

It was Raymond's first visitor since he returned from the VA hospital. His Harley and all his worldly goods had been stashed here during his psychiatric evaluation. He was detoxified, diagnosed with battle fatigue, and sent home with a bag of pills. Some of them made him sleep at night, and some calmed him down during the day, but in the end, his wits were so dull that he no longer cared whether he lived or died. Booze seemed simpler.

"Yeah, I'm back here. Come on in if you can stand the place."

"You living in here?"

"Welcome to my universe," Raymond said, sweeping his arms wide. "It doesn't look like much, but it's a lot better than some of the places I've lived in the past few years. Can I help you?"

"Sorry. My name is Clarence Biederman. My wife, Vernie, passed away a few months back. We had a farm north of town. She worked as hard at it as I did. I'm too old to farm it alone, so I'm selling out and moving to town."

"Look, I only have a toilet and cold running water, so this isn't a Holiday Inn."

"No, no, I've got a place to stay. That's not why I'm here. We've been living off what I make building cabinets. I'm looking for a place to set up a shop. I'm selling off everything on the farm, but keeping my woodworking equipment. Lou Baxter said I ought to come over here and talk to you."

"Lou sent you?"

"Yes, sir, he did."

"What else did he tell you?"

"That's about it. Said you was back from the war and having a hard time of it and that we might be able to help each other out."

"He didn't tell you that he wouldn't hire me back in my old job?"

"I don't recollect him saying anything about that. What kinda work did you do?"

"I was a reporter."

"Why wouldn't he hire you?"

"He said, and I quote, 'This town is too small for me to take a risk on a drunk.'"

"You too, huh?"

"What do you mean?"

"I was in World War I. I got all shot up at Argonne. I had a problem with the bottle after coming home too. Still do. It took me half my life to learn how to stay away from it. That's why I needed to farm, and that's why I need to build cabinets."

"Look, Clarence ... that's it, right? Clarence?"

"Yep."

"Can I offer you a cup of coffee? I only swiped one mug from Dutch's, but I can transfer this into a soup can or something and let you use the mug."

"Tell you what, why don't we go out for breakfast. I'm buying. I have a proposition for you."

Raymond didn't know what to think of Clarence until he saw him in action at Dutch's diner. Several people spoke to him on sight, expressing their condolences about Vernie. A contractor fished delicately to learn whether Clarence would be available to do the cabinets on his current building project. He would need him in another week or so. It soon became apparent that Clarence was well thought of and had enough work coming his way to be taken seriously.

"Here's the thing," Clarence said, cutting his waffle into uniform squares, "I need a small factory-like setup. Lumber and hardware delivered at one place, finished cabinets ready for pickup and delivery at another. I could use one bay for materials, cutting, planing, and shaping, put the jointers and clamps across the back wall, put a spray booth in the back corner, and use the end bay for storage and delivery of finished jobs. My shop at home isn't half as big, so this would be a major improvement."

"Yeah, but the hydraulic lifts are in the way. I don't know how to remove them."

"I already thought about that. It would be easier to build a plywood platform above them, level with the floor in the office."

"What about the weight of the equipment, like the drill press and saws?"

"Sonny, every shop has to have a floor. I can either load an existing floor up with machinery to see if it collapses or rest floor joists on a solid concrete slab. Get the floor level and solid, and the tools and jigs will be level and solid. Right now, I spend as much time shimming up my equipment as I do in production."

"I know it's nothing to look at, but it's the only place I have to live. So far, I've heard why it's a great idea for you, but what's in it for me?"

Clarence watched Raymond's eyes while he took a sip of coffee. Every deal had a crucial moment. This was it. He maintained eye contact and chose his words carefully.

"First, this can be a moneymaker for you. I pay you $100 a month rent, cover all the utilities, and you still get to live there. Second, I take the office area and turn it into living quarters for you, complete with hot water and a shower stall. Put in some windows, an efficiency kitchen, and build a shed out back where you can lock up your bike. Third, I'll paint the place inside and out for the privilege of putting up a sign that says 'Biederman Cabinetry.' You get proper living quarters, and I get live-in security to keep my machinery from getting stolen. That's what you tell the building inspector when he comes around saying the place is zoned commercial, not residential.

"Fourth, I'll hire you to help me handle material, loading and unloading, stuff like that. And when I get too old to work, there you sit, a landlord with a complete cabinet shop just waiting for the next guy to buy me out. I know it ain't much, but that's what's in it for you."

Raymond knew when he had just been hustled. Clarence might be old, but he wasn't stupid. Grinning with admiration and faced with the first hopeful prospects in years, Raymond reached out his hand to shake on it.

"Mr. Biederman, you have a deal. But I want you to know I let you off easy this time because you bought breakfast."

Clarence smiled and took note of something he would never say aloud. *I believe a partnership has just been formed.*

Biederman started calling in favors from his friends in the building trade. Some leftover paint, scrap lumber, a couple of used window casings, a little wiring and plumbing, and the shop ceased to be the blight it had been on the community. A painter sprayed the outside of the building a creamy off-white. The red and black lettering on the "Biederman Cabinetry" sign stood out blocks away.

True to his word, Clarence built an eight-by-ten lean-to behind the office for the bike with a sliding door where once a window pane had stood. The single step up to the brick window sill was an architectural oddity, but it served its purpose.

Helping Clarence lift the heavy equipment was made easier by the clever use of heavy-duty casters mounted on plywood sheets. Clarence placed the equipment in an unusual way. Instead of just dropping things where they would fit, Clarence waltzed through a pantomime of cabinet building. He started with enough room-to-handle four-by-eight sheet stock at the table saw, gradually working down to one or two paces between stations and opening up again at the other end to accommodate assembled units.

"It's hard to be efficient," he explained to Raymond, "when every job includes a five-mile hike. It's something I learned from years of farming."

By the time of the Well Stone Writing Festival in June, Biederman Cabinetry was in full production, and Raymond's life had structure. He was well muscled and sober and becoming increasingly interested in carpentry. Clarence taught him a little bit about assembly but insisted on doing all the cutting and finishing himself.

"Someday, I might teach you how to cut, but don't ever expect to finish one of my cabinets. A badly cut job never heals itself, but a poor finish on a perfect cabinet will always disappoint the customer and make trouble at the bank."

In the process of taking in a tenant, Raymond encountered one of the best possible incentives to avoid a hangover. Not long after Clarence opened the shop, Raymond went on a bender. The next morning, he was jolted out of bed by the god-awful sound of a table saw ripping half-inch plywood. It persisted throughout the pain of a cold shower, getting dressed, and brewing his morning coffee. When he finally stumbled out the front door, squinting against the sun, he got an annoyingly cheerful greeting from Clarence.

"Good morning, Sunshine. Hope I didn't wake you. It's gonna be a hot one, so I figured we'd better get the cutting done early."

A fellow might almost think it was intentional.

Chapter 21

▼

Well Stone Writing Festival

Friday, June 26, 1970

The interview with the agent for Simon & Schuster had not gone well. From what Raymond could deduce, he walked in with two strikes against him. The war was a gaping wound still tearing the nation apart, and most publishers were uncertain of the viability of that market.

More significantly, he had hammered it out at night on a battered Smith Corona with a worn-out ribbon. Never the neatest writer, he had grown careless during the war years. His manuscript contained strike-outs of whole passages because he tended to edit as he wrote. He really didn't have a manuscript. It was more like a set of working notes for the first draft.

Foster, the typesetter at the *Journal-Messenger*, had been far too forgiving. He could make sense of hopelessly ragged copy and set the type faster than most skilled typists could cut a clean copy. Not until this meeting did Raymond realize how much he had relied on him.

The agent had been polite, but it was obvious that Raymond would have to earn the right to be read. It was like building a cabinet. It was futile to show the framework to the customer when it still didn't look like anything. It was best to wait until the job was finished and installed in the best possible light. Yet it wasn't all bad news. Simon & Schuster was about to launch *Touchstone* and *Fireside Group* to publish paperbacks unsuitable for mass marketing.

"Perhaps your chronicle of the war will interest them. However, I do not presume to speak for them. You'll have to submit a far more presentable manuscript. But thank you for coming. Miss Carnahan, you may send in the next person."

Raymond's blood was boiling as he was shown out of the hotel room. He felt like a schoolboy who had been rebuked for accidentally barging into the teachers' lounge. The difference was that his project was not written by a schoolboy, but a man struggling with murderous rage. His first inclination was to go find some Scotch. That was when he deliberately set off toward the courthouse square instead, hoping for some distraction. The street vendors were set up on the bricks of Main Street, and all of Raleigh County seemed to be looking at the wares.

"Hey, look! It's Uncle Ray!" He turned to see Willie Grayson plowing through the legs of startled adults as he tore toward him, his sister, Meredith, squealing along behind. Raymond sank to one knee and put down the manuscript box, holding his arms out wide for them. It was just what he needed.

Betty Ann beamed when she saw him hugging her children and worked her way through the crowd toward him in her delicate and graceful way.

"Hi, Raymond," she said, bending down to give him a peck on the cheek. "It's good to see you. How have you been?" She had such a calming way about her.

"Things are going well, Betty." He stood up, resting a hand on each of the children's heads. They had each claimed a leg. "Clarence has so many jobs going that I can hardly keep up. He teaches me something new every day. I go to bed exhausted but satisfied. So how's my Piggly-Wiggly princess?"

"Oh, stop it! You know how that embarrasses me. I go to bed worn out too, but I am happy. Wally got promoted to frozen foods and loves what he is doing. He is going to meet us in a little while for dinner. Then we'll take the kids to the 'Liars Club.' Do you want to join us?"

"If you don't mind, Betty, I'd love that. Thanks."

They had turned together to walk towards the courthouse when Meredith tugged on his hand.

"Unko Way, is dat your box?" she said pointing at the sidewalk behind them.

"Omigosh, yes!" he said turning back.

"I get it! I get it!" shouted Willie, ripping off through the forest of adult legs. He was back in no time, holding the box out to Raymond with both hands.

"It's heavy. What do you gots in there?"

"Uncle Ray has been writing. That's what's in there."

"Will you read it to us?" Meredith asked.

"Not this, sweetheart. You wouldn't like it. It's not a children's story."

"Oh, pooh."

"Meredith! I have warned you about that, young lady," Betty said sternly, but a smile gave her away. She turned toward Raymond and shaded her eyes from the setting sun with one hand.

"Glad to hear you're writing again. What is it?"

Raymond's face clouded. He didn't know how to tell her. It seemed like another time, another life, another planet.

"It's the truth about Vietnam—all of it that I have to tell, anyway."

Betty's cheerful expression faded for a moment, but then she regained her poise.

"Good. Someone has to tell it. That thing at My Lai—"

"I know. And that's just the part the public knows. I am trying to tell the stories of guys who aren't around anymore. Millie said to write it down or die. It's hard to do, but better than night sweats."

An awkward silence fell between them. Willie and Meredith looked downcast. Betty cocked her head and looked at Raymond for a moment and then stepped in toward him and rested her hand over his heart.

"Good," she said and patted him twice. "Let's go get something to eat." No one else but Betty could have gotten away with it.

Two weeks later

"Why me? Typists are a dime a dozen," Millie said.

"Because I need proofreading help as well, and nobody is better at it than you. I'm serious about getting it published, Millie. You told me to tell their stories. I can do it without your help, but it won't be anywhere near as good."

"Nearly as good."

"What?"

"It won't be nearly as good."

"That's what I am trying to tell you."

"Wait a minute. Did you do that on purpose?"

Raymond stood with arms folded across his chest, leaning against the pillar on her porch with a twinkle in his eye.

"No. Of course you didn't. You're not that clever."

Raymond laughed. "See? That's why I need your help." Then slowly, the earnestness in his eyes returned again.

"I feel like I owe it to them to tell it right. And, well …"

"Well, what?"

"I'm scared, Millie."

"Of what?"

"I'm scared I won't do them justice. I owe them. I'm alive because of some of those guys. There was this one guy I could have killed myself if I had the chance. But when he dove on top of a hand grenade to save me, I fell apart. I just crawled in a hole and bawled. Crazy as it sounds, that stuff happened regularly."

Millie took a sip of her ice tea as she mulled over what he had just said. She pushed the front-porch swing back and forth slowly with the toe of one foot, the chain on the swing acting as a squeaky metronome. Clarence had taught him to recognize this moment as the one that determined whether a deal would be made. He waited silently.

"Okay. I'll do it. But only on one condition."

"Name it."

"You don't let me keep you from telling everything. If it's bloody or gory, tell it anyway. If it's ugly or profane, tell it anyway. Share their lives, every detail. Right down to the whores. Tell the whole story, Raymond, and tell it truly. Otherwise, I won't be helping. I'll be getting in the way of what you have to do."

"Are you sure about that?"

"I hope so. But I have to tell you something, Mr. Thornton."

"What?"

"Now we're both scared."

Chapter 22

A Soldier's Heart

Thursday, September 10, 1970

The sunset made the trees look like they were on fire. Millie sat on the porch swing wrapped in a quilt Mama Rosa had given her before she died. Rosa had postponed going to the nursing home far longer than was wise, and her falls had become more frequent. When Millie figured out that her landlady didn't have the money, she offered to buy the house. It came with Rosa's piano and her favorite quilt. Millie took great comfort in both of them.

A mug of tea sat on the porch railing; it had long since cooled. Millie's reading glasses were balanced on the tip of her nose as she read the manuscript and made notations in the margins. Millie understood why double-spacing was the standard for manuscripts. She had a lot to say.

Her notes were not so much criticism or corrections, but things she needed to ask Raymond. Millie concluded a long time ago that, having never experienced combat, her questions were probably typical of many other potential readers. Some things would matter in the telling of the story. Some things would not. But neither she nor Raymond would know which was which until she asked.

Raymond's tale was often so chilling that she had to seek out bright, sunny places to read it. She needed to surround herself with life in order to face a narrative about killing. Through it all, she was beginning to understand.

She discovered the real objective of a search-and-destroy mission. It was to return alive with as many of your buddies as possible. Washington may have had one idea of the objective. The theatre commander may have had another, and the brigade and company commanders yet another. But for the guys who went out into the jungle, it was all about sticking together, keeping each other alive, and making it back home to *the world*.

Millie sighed, put her reading glasses on top of her head, and stretched. She reached over for her tea and was surprised to find it cold. She drank it anyway.

There wasn't anything wrong with what she had been reading, but she wondered if it propelled the story forward. There was a boundary between writing for therapy and writing a compelling piece of literature. It was her job to keep Raymond on the right side of that boundary. The challenge was to frame the question in the right way so that he would consider her suggestions. Most of the time, it worked.

In the distance, she heard the sound she had been waiting for. It was the only Harley in town. She noticed that her pulse quickened and her spirits rose. *How interesting,* she thought as she dashed inside.

A pot roast simmered in the Dutch oven, and everything else in the refrigerator was ready to set out except for the dinner rolls. They had risen nicely on the cookie sheet and were ready to pop in the oven. She lit the oven and turned the dial to 400 degrees. She stepped out on the porch just as Raymond shut down the bike and dismounted.

"I brought some ice cream and chocolate syrup for later," he said. "I had to ride fast to keep the exhaust from melting it."

He dug into a saddlebag and retrieved a brown paper sack. He handed it to Millie. When she looked inside, she saw a quart-size carton from the Dairy Queen and a can of Hershey's chocolate syrup.

"Oh, how thoughtful! We'll put that to good use later," she said, heading toward the door to put it in the freezer. "Come on in and have a seat while I get supper on the table. Tell me about your day."

As Millie slid the rolls into the oven, Raymond took his mug off its hook, filled it with coffee from the percolator, and sat down.

"Clarence's hand looked worse today. It's all angry and red. I told him it looked infected and I thought he needed to go see Doctor Brown. He finally let me take him in. They gave him a tetanus shot and a bunch of pills."

"Is he all right?"

"As arrogant as ever, but he'll be fine. I don't think he will be doing any more cutting for a while. It is maddening to have him hovering over me when I am trying to cut a job, but everything he says is worthwhile. I just never knew it could be so hard to learn so much."

"Did you get any writing done last night?"

"Yep. I think I have finally gotten chapter eleven unstuck. But I'm not going to say anything. I'll just let you read it. How about you?"

"I liked what I read this evening. I made some notes. It's good. I just don't know if this is where it belongs in the book."

"Explain."

"Okay. Here's what I am thinking. The assault on Anh Khe is intense and complicated. It covers a lot of pages, but the writing is tight and there's not a lot that can be edited down. I'm just worried that it may be too early in the book for a reader to endure. If it gets overwhelming, the book could get tossed in the trash. Do you think your reader is ready to stick with you all the way through?"

"Are you saying it bogs down?"

"Good heavens, no. Your description of combat moves rapidly. But you and the other guys were stuck there. You had no choice. You had to fight it out or die. It's different for the reader. They can always put the book down and go bowling. I just don't think you want them to do that."

"Hmm. We keep having this discussion. I write for me, and you want me to write for the reader. Seems like we are at cross-purposes."

"Exactly. I think your book deserves to be read. The alternative is to go down to Driscoll's and buy a million copies yourself. But you decide. It's your book."

It had become a familiar scene for the Bartletts next door. On Tuesday and Thursday nights, Raymond would come to dinner. Through the dining room window, they could be seen laughing, talking, and having spirited debates. After the meal, they would clear away the dishes and pull two chairs together. There they would sit, looking at the three-ring binder that Millie kept and talking things out until Millie typed. Around nine thirty, they would scoot the chairs back and visit while cleaning up the kitchen and doing the dishes.

By ten o'clock, they were on the porch saying good night, then Millie would walk Raymond out to the bike. He would hand her some legal tablets, and after a cursory hug, he would fire up and ride off. But tonight was different. They sat together shivering on the porch swing. Raymond was the first to mention it.

"You know, to watch us on Tuesday and Thursday nights, somebody might think we were married."

"You'd better explain yourself, Mr. Thornton," Millie said with mock seriousness. *My God. Listen to me. I'm actually flirting.*

"Okay, I come home after work. You have dinner ready. We eat and talk about our days. Then we start arguing about the book, and it goes on for hours. Then we do the dishes together, say good night, I get a little hug, and we go off to separate bedrooms and go to sleep. We might as well be married."

Millie laughed and gave him a shot to the ribs. He doubled over and said, "See? I rest my case."

They held eye contact for quite a while, searching each other for any indication.

"You said you 'come home.'"

"What?"

"You said you 'come home.' Is that how it feels to you?"

He thought for a moment. "Yeah. That's how it feels."

"So, how do you like it?" Millie finally asked softly.

"Two nights a week, I like it."

"Which two?" she teased. "Friday and Saturday?"

"No," he said, looking earnestly into her eyes. "Tuesdays and Thursdays."

He brushed her cheek with the back of his fingers and put his arm around her shoulders. Millie leaned into him. Then she raised her head and kissed him.

"Wow," he said.

"What?"

"I never dreamed I'd get to do that. But I have wanted to ever since …"

She kissed him again and said, "Since what?"

"Since you first showed up on a load of watermelons."

Millie gasped then laughed aloud, fingertips raised to her lips. When her laughter ceased, her eyes still sparkled. She swept a loose strand of hair behind her ear, snuggled in close, and whispered, "Well, hello there, sailor. Let's try that again."

The next kiss was different.

"Arnold, come see this!"

"Come see what?"

"Millie and Raymond are kissing."

"No foolin'? Turn out the kitchen light, Molly. I'm coming." She heard the rattle of newspaper followed by the sound of Arnold shuffling along the plastic hall runner.

By the time he got to the kitchen, she had the light off. They stood side by side watching through the window of the breakfast nook.

"So what do you think?" she asked softly.

Arnold put his arm around her and said, "I think it's about damn time. Let's leave them alone and hope it takes."

The Second Wedding

June 15, 1973

A Soldier's Heart hit the book stands just in time for the Well Stone Writing Festival. It was published not by Simon & Schuster, but by Berkley Books, a recent acquisition of G. P. Putnam's Sons. The timing could not have been better. The U.S. had been negotiating an end to the war for nearly two years. On February 12 of that year, the first of 591 POWs returned to American soil in Operation Homecoming. The nation shared a collective sigh of relief.

It was the beginning of the end. The fall of Saigon was still two years off, but the nation was enduring the throes of political recriminations. Americans were beginning to ask what had been done to our young men and women, and *A Soldier's Heart* told them.

Sales started slowly at first, but by the end of the summer, it was a runaway bestseller. The author, a decorated combat veteran and recipient of a battlefield commission, went back home to make cabinets in a little town called Raleigh. Something about that resonated throughout America. But that was not the only thing that happened that year.

Just five days before *A Soldier's Heart* hit the bookstores, Margaret Millicent McKenna and Raymond Reginald Thornton Jr. were married at the First Presbyterian Church of Raleigh. Raymond asked Clarence Biederman to be best man. They had to trade places. Clarence moved into the shop, and Raymond moved in with Miss Millie.

Millie asked Mavis Baxter to be her matron of honor. The story that Lou accidentally caught the bouquet made it into the *Journal-Messenger*. Millie swore Pastor Cecil and the entire wedding party to secrecy about the twelve-year difference in their ages. It didn't seem to matter to anyone in Raleigh.

Chapter 23

▼

Back to the Weber Place

Thursday, July 10, 1975

Clarence and Raymond stood at the edge of the road looking at a shell of a house sinking into an ocean of weeds.

"No tellin' what we'll find when we start tearing into it. We may have to take it down to the footings. A place stands vacant like this, rats and termites have a picnic. This is a mess. How long you figure it has stood vacant?"

"Clarence, as far as I know, it has been empty since 1959."

"Was it livable then?"

"Yep."

"So how did it manage to end up like this?"

"A kid named Donny Weber was hanged in that barn back there. His father found him and cut him down. He was naked as a jaybird. I guess no one has wanted to live in a place with a memory like that. Can't say I blame them."

Clarence whistled and took off his feed cap to rub his scalp. Then he put it back on and twisted it into place. He was thinking about the eccentric college teacher who bought the land for a song.

"Well, no wonder Professor Grundig said to take it down to the ground."

Raymond reached into the bed of the truck and pulled out the double-edged weed cutter. Then he retrieved Clarence's .22 revolver from the glove box. He thumbed the release and flipped open the cylinder. It was a nice little Charter Arms Pathfinder with a short barrel.

"What have you got in this thing, twenty-two longs?"

"Yep. Why? You goin' huntin'?"

"Snakes. You have any snake-shot?"

"Yeah. There's a box of CCI/Speer in there. You worried about a few snakes?"

"You bet, Clarence. I have nightmares about the jungle. If I'm not killing VC, I'm killing snakes."

He ejected five rounds and tossed them into the glove box. He fed six rounds of snake shot into the cylinder, snapped it closed, and stuck the gun into his front pocket with the grip exposed. Clarence watched him carefully.

"You know, I always leave the hammer over an empty chamber myself, just in case I drop the gun."

"Coupla things wrong with that, Clarence. First, don't ever drop a gun. Second, it's just as easy to pull the trigger by accident. Then what? It's just as bad. Finally, this is a six-gun, not a five-gun. When it comes to snakes, you can never have too many bullets. Some people put their safety in the gun. I put it in my head. Let's go."

As they chopped their way down the driveway, Raymond answered questions about Donny's death. They took turns swinging the weed cutter back and forth to clear a trail wide enough to get the pickup through. When they had hacked their way into the shade of a white oak, they took a breather to cool off a bit.

That was when Clarence asked, "How come you know so much about it?"

"He was just a kid, not much younger than Wally and Bud and me. It looked to a lot of folks like he was murdered. His daddy thought so.

The sheriff and undertaker screwed up the investigation, so the three of us set out to catch the killer. We were just kids. But actually, Donny's old man asked us to do it. That was after he blew Wally's fingers off and I cracked his ribs."

"Whoa, whoa, whoa! You're going a little too fast for me."

"You don't know this story? I'm surprised! It was in the paper."

"Farmers only take city papers to light fires with, son."

So Raymond started at the beginning. He told Clarence all about that night.

"See that old toolshed over there?" he asked when he finished. "My Scout flashlight is still out there in that blackberry thicket somewhere. When the deer bolted, I fell over backwards. Bottom line is Wally lost his fingers and Bud lost his toes all on account of me. I let my buddies down," Raymond said, lapsing into that thousand-yard stare he got sometimes. Clarence studied him for a time before he spoke.

"How old were you then?" Clarence asked quietly.

"I don't know, fourteen, I guess. Why?"

"Son, your first combat didn't happen over in Vietnam. It happened right here. You realize that? Cut yourself some slack. A bunch of empty-handed kids go up against a fool with a shotgun. Everybody lives, and wasn't nobody left behind. Boy, you done good! So don't start up with the 'woulda-shoulda-couldas.'" Clarence extended the handle of the weed cutter toward Raymond's chest and said, "Take this damned thing and go find me a house."

As Raymond hacked his way up onto the front porch, he got a whiff of a cucumber-like smell. He was searching the ground when the old man joined him.

"Copperheads," Clarence said. The mushy boards yielded underfoot.

"Yep. Maybe under the porch. Hope they clear out before we start tearing this place down."

The house was a shambles. Windows were broken out, and rotting mattresses lay on the floor. It was plain that not even drifters would live here anymore. The ceilings had caved in, and the living room floor looked like a roller coaster.

"This makes it easy," Clarence said. "Nothing worth saving. We can get a skid-loader in here to pull her down to the ground, pile it over against the barn, and burn it."

"I've got a better idea."

"What's that?"

"Don't have one fire. Have two. Burn the house where it stands. Fire is free. A dozer isn't. Save your money to bury the rubbish."

"I like that. It's quicker and safer in the long run. Looks like Grundig will get his wish."

They stood on the porch staring in at the sagging floor.

"I don't even want to think about walking across that floor in there."

"Aw, go ahead, Clarence. Nothing here but copperheads and rats."

"You really got a thing about that, don't you?"

"Damn right I do."

"Okay, well, let's go to town. We know what it's gonna take now."

The Burning

Saturday, July 19, 1975

Word gets around in a small town. By the time the Raleigh Fire Department and the Coalmine Area Volunteer Fire District set up a training exercise, the local scroungers had gone to work. A scrap-metal outfit claimed all the rusty tractor parts out of the barn and most of the tin off the roofs.

It was a perfect fire exercise. The reality about rural fires is that by the time most volunteers get there, it is out of control and likely to involve fields and outbuildings. The goal is often containment instead of saving the property. The chiefs made one concession to a planned training event. They hired a local farmer to bring in his big John Deere with a sidebar and cut two swaths around the lot. Then they had him turn the soil over with a plow.

By 7:30 AM, two tankers were in the driveway, and two pumpers were out by the pond. The winds were light and variable so Clarence and Raymond lit the fires. Cars lined the ditch in both directions for a quarter mile. Millie was there, along with Lou Baxter, Wally, and the latest candidate for sheriff, Bud Oswald. As they watched human tragedy swirl into the sky in a cloud of black smoke, they sipped coffee and reflected on what it all meant.

"It's like another memorial service for Donny," Raymond said, choking back tears.

He hiked off into the woods to regain his composure. Millie watched him go in that soft way she had, her eyes also glistening in the morning sun.

"I've seen everything here I need to see," Wally said. He turned toward his car where Betty Ann sat with Willie and Meredith. Bud took all this in without appearing to notice. But mostly, he was searching the crowd for anyone who seemed out of place. One figure caught his eye. A big hulk turned and lumbered off when he saw Bud looking at him. He rolled to his right every time he swung his unbending left leg forward. The furtive glances over his shoulder made Bud ask himself why Brick Donovan would slink away from an intentional fire. There was no ready answer.

That was when Millie and Raymond volunteered to make a hamburger run. Handling bags of hamburgers for the firefighters would be easy. The trick was to figure out how to transport sixteen cokes without turning them over. Raymond hit on the idea of stacking them in a five-gallon bucket Clarence had in the back of his pickup. It worked.

All afternoon, Raymond had been replaying that night. He held Millie's hand as he strode from place to place, describing to her each event in precise detail. Of course, she had already heard the story, but she let him tell it again as though it was new. What she saw in Raymond troubled her. He appeared to be obsessing again and blaming himself.

By mid-afternoon, the house was gone and the barn was settling fast. By nightfall, the flames were spent; two red heaps of coals marked the landscape where the house and barn had stood. Most of the weeds burned clear, and even the old toolshed had been allowed to burn.

Dutch's diner was busier than usual that evening. People in Raleigh tended to gather there for unusual occasions. This was one of them. The Baxters were there, Mavis and Lou and their children, Danny, Donny, and Dot. So were the Graysons. Willie and Meredith shared a table with the Baxter kids while Wally and Betty Ann sat at the adjoining table with Lou and Mavis. Millie and Raymond were sharing a nearby booth with Clarence and Bud.

"Sheriff," Clarence said a little louder than necessary, "Raymond here told me you guys had some mighty interesting experiences out at the Weber place."

Bud winced, and Millie noticed.

"Now, Clarence, you know the election hasn't happened yet, so don't call him sheriff. You have to wait until after he's won." Her eyes twinkled. She knew Clarence well enough to know he was up to something.

"Well, I don't see why not," he replied even louder. Then he stood in a half-crouch and looked around the restaurant. "Everybody in here knows he's the best man for the job. Ain't that right, folks?" He got a chorus of "That's rights," "You betchas," and one "Damn straight" from the surrounding tables.

Clarence sat down with a grin, pointed his fork at Miss Millie, and said loudly, "So we might as well start callin' him sheriff now so's he'll remember it when he pulls us over for speedin'."

Millie laughed aloud. Bud grinned, shook his head, and put down his cup of coffee.

"I can tell you one thing, old man."

"Oh? What would that be?"

"The next time I pull you over, I am pretty sure I will remember this. And when I'm done, so will you!"

Clarence guffawed happily with a mouth full of fried chicken, and a chorus of catcalls ran around the room.

Dutch called over his shoulder. "You might as well sell that pickup, Clarence. Looks like you're walking from now on."

Clarence made people laugh. As the banter went on around him, Raymond smiled, but he was listening from a vast mental distance. It was familiar. It sounded like the guys in his unit giving each other a hard time while they sat on their duffle bags waiting for something—anything.

It's not Raleigh I love so much as it is all these people, he thought. *I haven't felt this much love since I was in Nam.* Tears welled in his eyes again. He blinked them away, concentrating on his ice tea.

Millie noticed a wet streak on his cheek and wiped it with her napkin as naturally as if she were shooing a fly. Somehow, she could do that drawing far less attention than if Raymond had done it himself. Then she gave him a playful bump with her shoulder.

In the car on the way home, she decided to confirm her suspicion.

"It was hard for you to watch the barn burn today, wasn't it?"

"Yes and no. It's better to burn down the place and see it full of life again. But it feels like we're giving up on Donny. Can't solve the crime, so let's destroy the scene—like it never happened."

"Can you do that? Give up and pretend it never happened?"

"No."

"Why not?"

"We promised his dad the kid would get justice. So far, we haven't done it."

"How well did you know Donny?"

"We barely knew him. He died not long after we met."

"Raymond, may I make an observation?"

"Sure."

"You have been pretty emotional today over a kid you barely knew, more than one might expect."

"Now, come on, Millie. That's not fair."

"No, no. Wait a minute. I didn't say there was anything wrong with that. I'm just saying there is more behind it than grief over the death of a kid you hardly knew."

"Then, what is it?"

"I've been working on that all day. Is it possible that Donny's death stands for something?"

"Like what?"

"You tell me."

They drove in silence. Raymond negotiated the familiar streets on autopilot and was surprised to find himself pulling into the driveway. He stared straight ahead as he killed the lights and shut down the car. He sighed and slumped down in the seat.

"Sweetheart, I'm sorry if I have upset you," Millie said leaning over to kiss him on the cheek.

"I was just thinking."

"What about?"

"Something Clarence said last week. It fits with what you just asked me."

"What was that?"

"He said the night that Wally and Bud got hurt was my first experience in combat. I thought he was just being Clarence, but he was trying to tell me something too."

"What?"

"You're both right. I barely knew Donny. He was just the first kid I ever knew to have his future destroyed by violence. Since then, I have seen hundreds, thousands even, if you count both sides. And I did my share. It's just that none of it makes any sense."

"Raymond, the whole idea behind *A Soldier's Heart* was to speak for your lost buddies. Everyone who reads it comes away with the image of you watching Lucas die in your arms."

"Maybe so, Millie. But tonight, I realized something."
"What is it?"
"When I wrote the book I missed one."
"Donny?"
"Yeah."
"So what are you going to do about it?"
"I'm not sure yet. But we promised he would get justice, whatever that means."

Barbecue

Saturday, August 2, 1975

Millie had originally asked everyone over to their place, but Wally and Betty Ann said it would be easier to put the children to bed if everyone came over to their house instead. So the grown-ups were gathered around the barbecue pit in the backyard listening to the whippoorwills and talking in low voices. Willie and Meredith, who were supposed to be in bed, listened at an open window upstairs.

"So after all these years, what do we really know about it?" Raymond asked. "Wally, you've been here all along. You ever hear anything?"

"Rumors and gossip, that's all."

"Like what?"

"Like our Scoutmaster was queer. Did you know that?"

"Good Lord, no! Is that true, Bud?"

"Ben Carson? Yeah, it's true. It explained some things about his behavior, but he never did us any harm."

"Like him sandpapering our shoulders with his beard at Sand Creek?"

"Yeah. Stuff like that. But his record was clean. He just seemed to drift away from town a few years later."

"Was Donny in Scouts?"

"Not that I recall," Wally said. "He would have joined a year or so after we did, and I don't remember him being at any campouts. We got all the tenderfoots."

"Bud, I bet you have thought about this a lot. What do you think?"

"Well, the Webers were Catholic. The church had a priest that kept getting moved around in the fifties because he liked choirboys. No history of violence, just a real creep."

"Could something have happened that would make Donny commit suicide?"

"Who is Donny?' Meredith asked Willie at the window.

"Shush," Willie told her. He pressed a finger to his lips and whispered, "Don't talk. We'll get caught. We're just getting to the good parts."

"It doesn't fit," Bud said. "That kind of victim leaves a note. They can't live with the shame, and they want to blame their abuser. Donny was a happy-go-lucky kid who left no note."

"Donny's brother was sorta weird. What was his name?" Wally asked.

"Dillon … and his pal Cecil, Cecil Winters, who was a lot older. I could see them doing things. But Dillon was weak. He would have crumbled."

"Hmm," Raymond said, "do you think Papa hauled the family out of town to protect him?"

"Sure. He even told us that in so many words."

"Bud, whatever came of Dillon and Cecil?"

"I don't know for sure. We'd have to pick that trail up in Emporia."

"Who are Dillon and Cecil?" Meredith asked Willie.

"You kids get away from that window and go back to bed!" Betty Ann called out.

"Aw, gosh, Mom. We're not sleepy."

"Willie, Meredith, do you want a spanking?"

"No, ma'am," came the plaintive replies.

"Then get back in bed."

"Yes, ma'am."

They stood at the window and showed themselves as they walked off to the bedrooms. Meredith actually got in bed and went to sleep. Willie waited awhile before crawling back to the window on all fours where he hunched down below the sill, hugging his knees to his chest. Grown-ups had the coolest secrets.

Chapter 24

Going to Emporia

Wednesday, November 19, 1975

"Sheriff Oswald, this is Harlan Francis, police chief, Emporia, Kansas. Who the hell is Raymond Thornton and what is he doing nosing around in my backyard on a case for your department?"

"Hold on, chief. He's not one of mine. He's not even a law enforcement officer. He is a writer. I'll kill him for you when he gets back here if you like. Tell me what he's done so I can explain it dumb enough for him to get it."

Bud grabbed a pencil and started taking notes.

"Uhuh. Uhuh ... What? ... You've gotta be kidding me. He said that? ... Then what did he do? ... I understand. No, no, I don't mean I understand why he did it, I mean I understand your take on it ... No, no. It's quite all right ... I would have done the same thing ... Thanks for calling me and giving me the first crack at him ... I assure you it will not happen again ... No, sir, I wouldn't blame you if you did ... Yes, sir. Tank time actually sounds like a good idea. Have you got a reason to hold him until I can get someone there? ... Probably about this time tomorrow ... I appreciate it ... No, go ahead and gnaw on him all you want. Maybe it'll do him some good ... Thank you. I will take care of it, permanently ... Thanks again ... Good to talk to you too, sir ... Yes, sir. Good-bye."

Bud dropped the phone in the cradle, tossed the pencil onto the desk, and rocked his chair as far back from his desk as he could. He stared at the phone in disbelief. The heels of both hands rose to the sides of his head, and he took a deep breath. Suddenly, he slammed the desk with his fists hard enough to make coffee jump out of the mug.

"Son of a bitch!" he said. He rose and walked out into the dispatch area.

"Lucy, call Sam and tell him to come see me as soon as he can. I have a special assignment for him. Oh, but tell him to go by the library first and see if he can get a book by Truman Capote called *In Cold Blood*. I want to use it to beat the crap out of someone."

Less than a half hour later, Deputy Sam Whiteside knocked on the door frame to Bud's office. Bud waved him over to a seat while he finished up a phone call.

"Okay, Sam, here's the deal. It seems our local war hero, part-time town drunk, author, and carpenter, one Raymond Reginald Thornton Junior, has gotten his ass in the slammer in Emporia, Kansas. He claims he was working on a special assignment for this department as a personal favor to me—to solve the Weber murder in 1959."

"Well, was he?"

"Hell no! And since I've only been sitting in this chair for two weeks, I am not going to let this turn into a scandal. The chief of police, Harlan Francis, says they have grounds to hold him until we can get somebody there to pick him up."

"Why not just release him and let us pick him up when he gets back here?"

"That's what I would normally do, but he claimed to represent this department, and he is a friend of mine. So we have to investigate whether he was impersonating an officer. Folks here can't see me just slap him with a rolled-up newspaper and say 'bad dog.' If they are going to trust me, they need to see that a friend of mine gets no special treatment. That's your assignment."

"I'm with you. So what do you want me to do?"

"I want you to take my pickup truck to Emporia and collect him and his bike. My rig will haul his Harley with the tailgate down. I know, because I've done it before."

"Okay, I can do that."

"But when it comes time to head back, you sit him down in the bed and handcuff his ass to the engine guard on that bike. Let him take an eight-hour beating back there."

"What?"

"I don't care if it snows or rains. I don't care if you run through a hailstorm. In fact, you have my permission to drive out of your way to find one."

"Sheriff, he ain't going to like that. Do you expect him just to climb in there all peaceably and let me hook him up?"

"You are the biggest SOB in this department; you have my permission to be the meanest."

"And how's that going to look, me driving back here with him cuffed to his bike?"

"Anybody questions you, just explain we are a small department transporting a prisoner with the only resources we have. This may be the only chance we get to stop him from being an idiot. Any more questions?"

"Yeah. Let me see if I get this. I get to spend a couple days listening to the radio and driving cross-country?"

"Yes, you do, with per diem and mileage. Meanwhile, I have two days to do my homework. Did you find that book?"

"Oh, yeah. I have it right here." Sam slid the book onto Bud's desk.

"What's that all about?" he said, pointing at the cover.

"Chief Francis says that some law officers in Kansas hold a pretty dim view of authors since Capote made heroes out of two killers in a

Kansas murder case from 1957. I figure I'd better find out what he's talking about."

"Sounds interesting, Sheriff. I think I'm going to like this assignment."

"Listen, Sam. Thornton is a fighter. He is tough. Don't you let him get the jump on you, or I'll have to drive out there to fetch you back here myself."

Bud wrapped his thumb and forefinger around his chin and thought about what he just said.

"Listen, considering his history, maybe you should take someone with you. It would make a better explanation about why the prisoner was in back. Who would you take?"

"Cassius Green is my choice. He was in Nam, lifts weights, and looks real intimidating."

"Okay, Sam. You and Cassius are a team. Bring me Mr. Thornton, a little worse for wear, I hope, and sorry as hell for making the biggest mistake of his life."

Bud fished the keys out of his pocket and tossed them to Sam.

"Okay, that's about it. But let me ask you a different kind of question."

"Sure."

"I have to call Miss Millie. If you were going to do it, what would you tell her?"

"Let me call her, Bud. It will look better for you if I'm the one who calls."

"Okay, Sam. You've got it. Just don't get me killed, okay?"

Chapter 25

▼

The Return from Emporia

Thursday, November 20, 1975

Bud saw her coming through the door and had to fight the temptation to dive under his desk. She breezed past everyone and entered his office to stand before him.

"Miss Millie, it sure is a pleasure as always to see you."

"I appreciate your efforts to be professional, Bud, but this isn't pleasant for either one of us. I am pretty sure we need to compare notes. May I sit down?"

"Please, Millie."

"Sam Whiteside called yesterday just before leaving to go get Raymond. He explained why two deputies were going out there and that they were taking your truck to haul the bike back. But he didn't really give me any ideas about why Raymond was in jail. Can you fill me in?"

Bud weighed what he should and should not tell the spouse of a man who may or may not have been impersonating an officer. In the end, he decided it was Millie. So he let out a sigh and retrieved his notes from the phone conversation with Chief Francis.

"I got a call yesterday at 1:22 PM from the chief of police of Emporia, Kansas. He said that local residents reported being interviewed by a fellow claiming to be with the Raleigh County Sheriff's Department. He identified himself as Raymond Thornton and said he was assisting the RCSD in investigating the death of Donny Weber in 1959. He said he was doing it as a personal favor to me."

"Oh, good heavens, Bud! This is worse than I thought. I am so sorry."

"Millie, you have nothing to apologize for. Raymond, on the other hand, has a world of explaining to do. Did you know he was going to Emporia to do this?"

"He told me he was going to ride out there and see what he could learn about the Webers, but he didn't tell me much more than that."

"Well, things really went south on him when they picked him up. He began dropping my name, making it sound as if I had dispatched him out there. Chief Francis was blistered to have some outsider stomping on his grapes. Ever since Truman Capote wrote this," he said, holding up the library book, "cops in Kansas are not real fond of writers."

"*In Cold Blood.* I've read it. It's ghoulish. So what do you plan to do with Raymond?"

"Millie, he is one of my best friends, but I simply cannot allow him to take advantage of me or this office. I don't care how much we have been through together. I can't play favorites."

"What do you have in mind?"

"A little 'curbside justice.'"

"Bud, that doesn't sound good." Millie stiffened.

"I'm not talking about police brutality," Bud said, spreading his hands wide. "The truth is that when we get him back here, we probably won't have a case for impersonating an officer. It will come down to innuendo and inference, nothing concrete. But if I don't do something, he could get into far more serious trouble later on."

"Is this like a GI party?"

"Take him out behind the barracks and work him over with a bar of soap in a sock?"

"Is that what you have in mind?"

"Close."

"I see."

"When Raymond gets back here, he is going to be mad as hell at me. That's okay. But I don't want it to slop over on you. Do you have someplace you can go for a couple of days until he simmers down?"

"Just what do you have in mind?"

"Okay. Here it is. I sent my two biggest guys. I told them to watch out for each other because we know he can be dangerous."

"So far, so good."

"Raymond might test a single deputy, but he won't take on two."

"Okay. So exactly what is it that will make Raymond mad?"

"He isn't going to ride home sitting between deputies."

"No?"

"No. He is going to ride in the bed of a pickup, handcuffed to his damned Harley."

Millie gasped, her eyes opening wide. She studied Bud for a moment and then laughed out loud.

"Oh, Bud! You know how to get to him. You're right. Raymond will be mad. Mostly, he's going to be furious with himself for doing something so stupid."

"He will figure out exactly what I'm doing and why. And it is going to piss him off worse than a bobcat in a gunnysack. Millie, you may not want to be here when we dump him out on the floor."

Millie chuckled. Bud wore a crooked smile, not sure he found it as funny as she did. She caught her breath and looked him in the eye. She placed both hands on top of his. "Bud, with all his faults, Raymond is a good man. Sometimes he is misguided, but a good man. Get his attention. Just don't put him behind bars. Don't push him too far. That would kill us both."

For the first time in his life, Bud saw something in Millie he had never seen before—vulnerability. The thought of hurting her brought tears to his eyes.

"Millie, I love the guy too, even though he can be a complete jackass. This is twisting my guts out. But I know Raymond about as well as anybody, and this is the only play I've got."

"I have."

"What?"

"It's the only play I have, not the only play I've got."

"I'm talking about hauling your husband home in handcuffs, and you are correcting my English. You are amazing! Did you know that?"

"I know. I can't help it."

She let go of his hands and pulled a tissue out of a box on the desk. Bud dug into his back pocket for his handkerchief. Millie dabbed at her eyes. Bud blew his nose and put the handkerchief back.

"Where can you go for safety?"

"Right here."

"What?"

"Bud, if this is going to work, I have to be here with you when he arrives. In fact, the more witnesses the better."

"Millie, that's not exactly good police procedure."

"Neither is hauling a prisoner across two states with a motorcycle in his lap. Come on, Bud, you abandoned protocol on this a long time ago."

"So what do you suggest?"

"Get every deputy you have in here with us when he arrives. Bring in the dispatchers. Get Clarence and Wally and Betty Ann in here, and Lou Baxter too."

"What?"

"Clean out Dutch's Diner and bring everybody over here. Let Raymond try to explain himself to everyone in this town. And let him see a solid wall of people who love him saying, 'No more.'"

It was a strange suggestion, but the more Bud considered it, the better he liked it.

An Uneasy Distance

It was pretty clear who was sheriff and who was not. Still, a curious bond remained between them. Raymond may have been angry about being hauled into public accountability, but he admired Bud for doing it. Still, it changed the nature of the relationship forever.

Things were tense when Raymond and Millie got home that night. He sulked on the porch swing for over an hour. When Millie came out with two cups of tea and some cookies, he sat with his elbows on his knees and his fingertips pressed against his mouth. She sat down next to him and stroked the back of his neck. When at last he turned to look at her, she spoke.

"Raymond, I love you. Nothing changes that, so let's talk about it."

It took awhile. He had lots to say. He talked about his original intentions in going. He described finding Donny's headstone with Dillon's next to it, a casualty of war in 1965, a sergeant in the 1st Air Cavalry. Mr. and Mrs. Weber were there as well. Roger died in 1970, and Lillian three years later.

He rode away from the graveyard mulling it over. He passed a barbershop, and on a whim, he went in to see if anyone there could tell him where Roger Weber had cut hair. That was the chain of interviews that eventually got back to the police chief, and things went downhill from there. Eventually, he got around to the part that bothered him the most.

"What was Bud thinking? What was the big idea in bringing all those folks over to the sheriff's department? Is public humiliation a part of modern law enforcement?"

"He did it because I asked him to."

"You what?"

"Actually, it was an easy choice. Either watch you get prosecuted for impersonating a law enforcement officer or talk Bud into finding some other way to make you stop and think before doing something like this again."

"Well, it was unprofessional and totally uncalled for. Why would Bud do something like that?"

"I told you. It was because I begged him not to send you to jail."

"You did what?"

"Think about it. If you went to prison, it would destroy us. Bud was willing to forfeit a friendship so we can be together. He's the best friend you could ever want. And all those others who were there? They are your friends too. Every single one of them cared enough about you to show up."

"I have a hard time believing that."

"Is it so hard for you to believe that I'll do whatever it takes to be with you? I waited a long time for you, and I am not going to go through that again."

She rose up to kiss him on the cheek. They cried and laughed until she led him by the hand back into the world they inhabited together. It was good to have a home and friends.

Chapter 26

▼

Magnum Opus

Saturday, March 3, 1976

It took longer than anyone expected, but Clarence was a bulldog. A brand-new four-stall horse barn stood out back. It had a hayloft and a lean-to for the tractor and farm equipment. Clarence seemed as proud of it as the six-gable, two-story house that sat like a crown in the middle of the circular driveway. A four-car garage stood opposite the barn. It too was painted barn red with white trim to match.

The house, white with red trim, had a wide porch that wrapped around on three sides. The double-wide front door opened into a grand foyer with an elegant stairway that spiraled upward along a curving interior wall. Raymond had not thought it possible to make drywall curve like that, but Clarence knew tricks that had never been written down.

As they had stood in the foyer admiring the unwavering lines of the wall and the handmade staircase, Clarence told Raymond.

"Sonny, this is my last house."

"Not going to take on any more jobs this big?"

"No. Not that. I mean I am not going to be around much longer."

"Aw, come on, Clarence. When people see this, they are going to line up to get you to build them a house."

"Well, then, they are going to be real disappointed. I doubt that I'm going to see Thanksgiving."

"What?"

"Cancer of the pancreas. Doctor says there is no chance of a cure. It is starting to spread. So what you see is my legacy. That's why I have been so finicky."

Raymond slumped down on the steps and looked up at him.

"No, Clarence, there has to be some mistake."

Clarence took his hat off and rubbed his head.

"No, no mistake. And I just didn't want anybody making excuses for me by saying, 'Well, it was his last house.'"

Raymond looked away and asked, "How long have you known?"

"Since Christmas. Not a lot of choices. Spend a fortune to maybe add a few months to your life, so I decided to make something out of the time I had left. I'm right pleased, actually."

"But, what about the shop? What about the jobs we have lined up?"

"You'll do just fine. You don't need me anymore. I taught you everything I know, and a few things I don't. You figure out which is which."

"Well, we need to decide what the business is worth so I can buy you out."

"Now, listen, Raymond. I invested a lot of time in you. I thought it was a good bet. So you just keep things going like they are and you'll be fine."

"I know, but you're going to need the money."

"You could pay me a million dollars and it would all come back to you, at least the part that didn't get eaten up by lawyers and taxes. Vernie and me were all we had. You and Millie are my family now, except for maybe the half of Raleigh who pretends to like me. The others won't know I'm gone."

"Clarence, that's not true."

"I'm going to have you and Millie settle things up for me. If there's anything left over, you get it. So it don't make no sense for you to buy me out. First thing we'd know, you'd go get a bank loan. Next thing, they would try to tell you how to run the business. You don't need that."

"But ... how are you doing? I mean, are you having pain?"

"Oh, yeah. That's what made me go see Doc Brown. Started out I hurt after I ate. Losing weight, just like Millie thought. Now I hurt all the time."

"So, what is the treatment? Radiation? Chemo?"

"Nope. Waste of time and money. They try to kill you, but not quite. I wanted to work as long as I could. But I have to quit now."

"So what happens next?"

"I don't know. Nobody does. But I finish with the lawyer tomorrow and start throwing stuff away. I may even have time now to read your book."

By the first of April, Clarence was confined to a hospital bed in Mama Rosa's music parlor. The baby grand had gone to the fellowship hall at church. Raymond and Millie took turns staying up at night. Nurses covered the daytime.

By the time Holy week came, Clarence required morphine to relieve the pain. He died during the early hours of Good Friday. He spoke his last words the evening before.

"Vernie, I can't find my glasses. Read the paper to me, will you, hon?"

Millie read to him as he faintly smiled and went to sleep. She kissed him on the forehead and curled up in the chair to read.

He called out just after 3:00 in the morning. Millie rose to check on him. She found he was gone. She prayed, kissed his forehead one last time, and climbed the stairs to tell Raymond.

Under New Management

April 20, 1976

"How does this look, Raymond?"

"Make it bigger."

"How much bigger?"

"Big enough to read a block away."

"What do you think, maybe three times this size?"

"Yeah, Tater. That'll be good."

Tater Gilmore leaned out from the extension ladder and sketched freehand with a marker.

"You know, I can match the paint pretty close. I may not have to redo the whole sign."

"You got a problem with me paying you to repaint the whole sign?"

"Well, of course not," he answered, a smile flashing across his face.

"Can you get her done today?"

"Sure can."

"Then sling that paint, Tater. Sling that paint."

"That'd be fine, Raymond."

"Is Tater your given name?"

"Naw. It's Lucius."

"What do you want me to call you?"

"Everybody 'round here calls me Tater."

"All right, then. My given name is Raymond, but from now on, you can call me Sonny. Think you can do that?"

"Sonny? Sure, I can do that."

Raymond loaded three cabinet bases and two countertops into the pickup and opened the driver's door. He shielded his eyes against the sun and looked up at the ladder."

"Leave me a note telling me how much I owe you, and I'll have your check ready tomorrow. That okay?"

"No problem."

"Later, Tater."

"Funny, Sonny."

They grinned and exchanged waves, one driving away to install new cabinets, the other revising the layout of the sign.

The overhead cabinets were already in place, so setting the bases and counters was the last part of this job. As he worked on the installation, he could hear Clarence's voice. "Always, always, always install the overhead cabinets first. You can stand underneath to get them mounted right. And if you drop your hammer, you don't have to replace a whole countertop. Don't ask me how I know."

It still felt like Clarence was with him everywhere he went. He was just around the corner in the shop. He was just in the next room on the job. And he and Millie kept expecting him to join them for dinner at Dutch's. But he didn't scoot in beside Millie anymore.

The installation went smoothly thanks to the things Clarence had taught him. He drove by the house to see if Millie was home from school. She was grading papers at the dining room table.

"Honey, you want to go for a ride?"

"Sure. What did you have in mind?"

"Tater Gilmore repainted the sign today. I haven't seen it yet. You want to come along?"

"Oh, sure. Let me get my sweater."

Raymond turned the corner and stopped the car. They both got out and shielded their eyes to get a good look.

"Oh, Raymond! Clarence would love it!"

"Raymond? Who's Raymond?"

"Okay then, Sonny. Take a girl out to dinner to celebrate?"

The sign on the front of the shop announced new management:

BIEDERMAN & SON, CABINETRY
Raymond "Sonny" Thornton, Proprietor

Tater showed up after quitting time the next day. He wore painter's whites with blotches of every color under the sun. It was hot, and sweat ran down his mahogany face, tracking along the smile crinkles around his eyes and mouth.

"Hey there, Tater," Raymond called out from the office door. "Been expecting you. Come on in. You have time, don't you?"

"Sure. I got a few minutes."

"You want a soda? I've got some Pepsi in the fridge."

"Man, that sounds good."

Raymond walked over, opened the door, and snatched out a bottle. He pried off the cap and handed it to Tater.

"Here you go. Have a seat. Take a load off your feet. The sign looks great, even better than I expected."

"I'm glad. It's too hot to repaint it today."

Raymond reached across the desk and picked up a check stapled to Tater's invoice.

"You trying to pull a fast one on me here?" he said, holding the check out toward Tater.

"Oh, I'm sorry, Raymond. I didn't intend for it to cost that much. I can make an adjustment if you want me to."

"Tater, you didn't overcharge me. I think you undercharged. By my calculations, you were up on that ladder at least six hours yesterday. What do you mean only charging me fifty bucks?"

"I didn't want you to get mad at me."

"I figure with your skill, you're worth twelve bucks and hour, and I don't expect you to provide the paint. I've written a check here for a hundred dollars, and if you don't take it, I will get mad." He handed the check to Tater, whose face lit up with gratitude.

"Besides, I want to get some information out of you, so sit down and relax a bit. You have the time?"

"Sonny, for you, I have time."

"Good. Here's what I want to ask you. How is your cousin Larry doing? I haven't seen him since high school graduation?"

Tater's face fell. "Didn't you hear? He's dead."

"What? No! That can't be right."

"Yeah. About six or seven years ago now. Two guys in uniform drove an Air Force car up to Uncle Julius' to tell 'em. Chaplain and some second lieutenant, as I recall."

"What happened?"

"He was killed in a maintenance accident over in Thailand. They had an F-4 up on jacks. Some new kid raised the landing gear while Larry was working in the nose gear wheel well. Family had a closed casket funeral. He was crushed from the shoulders up."

Raymond sat back in horror, momentarily speechless. Then he covered his face with one hand and shook his head.

"Oh, Tater, that's such a shame. I had a great time with him in Chicago. We sneaked out at night to go to the jazz clubs. I'll never forget that."

"He used to talk about it. Did you guys actually meet Miles Davis?"

"Yeah. I had no idea who he was at the time. Larry recognized him and said, 'You look like that trumpet player Miles Something-or-other … Miles …?'

"The guy answers, 'Davis.'

"Larry grabs us by the arm and pulls us over to introduce us. Miles asks what two white boys were doing out with a black kid that time of night, and Larry says he brought us to hear real jazz. Miles says, 'The bar's closin' now. Why don't you guys come inside and listen to one of our sessions?'"

"No shit?"

"It's true. Coolest night of my life was spent with Bud and Larry. At that point, we didn't care if we got caught or not. What could they do? Kick us out of school?"

"Wait a minute. You mean Sheriff Bud?"

"Yep."

"Don't that beat all? The 'Man' himself cuttin' curfew an' groovin' on Miles. Guess he used to be cooler than we thought."

"Yeah, but it was Larry who was truly cool. He took a couple of white kids under his wing and taught us about improv. He was a good guy. I really like him—liked him."

"Wow. That's sumpthin'. Julius would enjoy hearing about it. He's old now and talks about Larry a lot. It would mean a lot to him to know about Chicago. You should go over and talk to him some."

"Really? You think that'd be all right?"

"I'm pretty sure he wouldn't have no problem with it. Would you?" Raymond smiled, scratched his neck, and gave it some thought.

"Naw. It's not a problem for me. As a matter of fact, it sounds like fun. Tell Julius I am sorry about Larry and might enjoy comparing stories one day. Will you do that, Tater?"

"Sure. I'd kinda like to sit in myself. But I gotta get going now. Thanks for the pop," he said, holding up the empty bottle. He put it on the counter by the sink and headed for the door.

"Good to see you. Thanks for the sign. Stop by to talk when you can."

"I'll do that," Tater said as he stepped back out into the heat. "And by the way, nice apartment you got here. Never knew you had living quarters."

"Security. Keeps folks from stealing the machinery."

"Somebody lives here?"

"I used to. Then Clarence did for awhile until he got so bad we had to take him over to our place. You know anybody who could keep an eye on things for me?"

"Not right off but let me think about it."

"You do that. It's private unless you have to tell some drunk to go somewhere else to pee."

"I'll get back to you. Thanks for the job and the soda," he said as he waved and let the door close.

I enjoy Tater almost as much as I liked Larry.

To the folks in the construction trade calling him "Sonny" came easily enough. Some even referred to him as "Sonny Biederman," not as much to identify him as to signify top-end cabinets.

Contractors used it as a form of shorthand. It was the kind of advertising money couldn't buy. The day Raymond learned about it, he realized the Grundig house was not Clarence's only legacy. That evening, he told Millie, "I heard something today you might find interesting."

"Really? What's that?"

"I was in Ace hardware, looking at their drawer pulls. Sid Waller was talking to Doc Brown the next aisle or so over. Looks like the Browns are going to remodel the kitchen and add on in back. So Sid says, 'Now, about the cabinets, how do you want to go? Do you want me to keep the price down, or do you want a set of Sonny Biederman's?'"

"Sid said that?"

"Yep. Those were his words. 'Or do you want a set of Sonny Biederman's?'"

"So what did Doc say?"

"He said, 'Oh, Martha would skin me if I didn't get her the best.'"

"Clarence would have enjoyed that."

"I could have sworn I heard him say, 'Well, whaddya know?' I turned to look for him, but no one was there. I've been chuckling about it all afternoon.'"

"Looks like you have something to live up to, buster."

"Isn't that the truth? A lot of guys have to live up to their father's expectations. Me? I have two of them."

"Are you complaining?"

"No. I figure I'm a pretty lucky guy."

"You sure are. You have me."

"My point exactly. See how lucky I am?"

Chapter 27

Firebug

Friday, May 21, 1976

The new sign did it. Brick Donovan discovered Raymond owned the cabinet shop. He began wondering what he could do with the new information. He had been a garbage collector since the shoe factory closed. Riding the trucks around Raleigh let him keep track of everyone's vices.

The dean of students at the college subscribed to *Playboy*. He didn't realize that Brick was on his hand-me-down list. One of the local ministers was fond of red wines, and another preferred cheap Scotch. The local wire chief drank Jack Daniel's and Busch Bavarian. In his trash, "Black Jack" was evident year-round, but beer was seasonal, coming and going with watermelon rinds and barbecue scraps.

When Mr. Diener had his stroke, it came as no surprise to Brick. He had been reading the prescription labels for over a year. It was satisfying to know the principal who kicked him out of school spent time in his own dull-witted hell before he finally succumbed.

He kept some things he fished out of the trash as evidence of private secrets, like the prom queen's empty pack of birth control pills. Some things he used as talismans, others like voodoo dolls. He used them to wish ill on those he despised. Many of his treasures were simply fuel for his fantasies.

Living alone meant he could take home whatever he wanted. After his mother died, the ramshackle house on Bluff Street looked abandoned, a circumstance that was fine with him. He lived in secrecy. No one knew his vices. He disposed of his own trash. The things that were most damaging could be discarded in the dead of night or tossed in the crusher at daybreak. It was the perfect job.

No one treated him as a human being. Neighbors looked away, choosing to know as little as possible about the man who hauled away their garbage. For Brick, the smells were a minor inconvenience compared to the goods he could get on his fellow residents. He knew who the local hypocrites were and whose private lives belied their public persona.

That was what infuriated him about Millie and Raymond. They simply were what they seemed—decent and hardworking. The empty Scotch bottles disappeared about the time Raymond's book got published. Perhaps the shop would yield more secrets than their home. Today he "accidentally missed" that block and returned to finish at the end of the day. No one noticed. No one cared. Working alone offered distinct advantages.

Brick realized the apartment was occupied when he saw the kitchen scraps. The only way to wind up with full-length corncobs in Raleigh was to cook them yourself. Dutch's Diner broke their cobs in half. Whoever it was favored fried chicken, fruit cocktail, and canned soup. It would be good to know who was living there.

A little after midnight, he drove his mother's '72 Plymouth station wagon down Fifth Street past Raymond's shop. It was too easy. He saw Tater Gilmore's work truck parked out front. All the lights were out, so he decided to take a closer look. He turned left into the next alley and left his car parked in shadows between the garages. It blocked the alley, but at this time of night, it wouldn't matter. It was better to be ready for a hasty exit.

Instead of walking up the sidewalk, he slipped along in the shadows back toward the shop. The front side of the building was exposed to the street, so he edged around behind. Against the back wall, he discovered a small addition like some sort of storage shed. Two of the three walls were unbroken. But the third, the one forming an ell with the main building, had a set of double doors that swung outward. A simple hasp and padlock held it closed.

Brick opened the screwdriver blade on his pocketknife and carefully backed out all four screws on the right-hand side of the hasp. When it was free, he pushed the left door in with his shoulder and curled his fingers around the inside of the right door. Pulling up with both hands, he lifted the door off the ground to keep it from dragging and to keep the hinges from squeaking. Carefully, he pulled the door open enough to stick his head in and take a look around with his penlight. At first, he saw only buckets of paint and scraps of lumber, but there, on the common wall, was what he was looking for: a doorway inside.

Perspiration burned in his eyes, but he concentrated as he lifted the door against the hinges and slowly closed it again. He inserted two screws through the hasp and tightened them just enough to hold everything in place. He tossed the two extra screws into the hedge behind the building. Then he straightened and listened carefully as his breathing returned to normal. He heard his heart pounding, but nothing else. He scuttled toward the alley as quickly as he could with one straight leg.

A dog on an enclosed porch heard him shuffling past and charged the screen door, barking and lunging. Soon, dogs up and down the street had joined in. Swearing and muttering under his breath, Brick reached the alley and lunged toward the car just as Tater, wearing nothing but boxers, stepped out of the front door to take a look around.

A car in the alley spun tires in the loose gravel and drove away. Tater stood for a long time after the car left with his head cocked, listening attentively. The barking died down. He couldn't see or hear anything, so he went back to bed.

Driving east on Fifth Street toward Bluff, Brick lit a cigarette and settled on a plan. The building was concrete block, so it would need at least five gallons of gasoline inside to do any good. That meant he had to wait somewhere until the nigger was gone. Then he could go in through the shed, break in the back door, douse everything with gas, lay a trail back outside, flick a cigarette, and enjoy the show.

In, out, and up in flames in less than five minutes. Then Raymond Thornton, the hotshot who got him kicked out of school and left him maimed for life, would know what it was like to be without a livelihood. If another Gilmore boy got messed up in the process, well, it served them all right for acting like they were as good as whites. He started looking forward to it. *Sunday night. Let's get her done.*

It was nearly midnight when Millie and Raymond got in, sunburned and weary from the canoe trip. But it had been great. They had spent two days camping and floating down the spring-fed rivers before the busy season began, spotting flying squirrels, great blue herons, otters, deer, and turkeys. They saw snakes too, but the weather was mild and the water cold, so they tended to be sluggish. It didn't matter. Raymond had insisted on carrying Clarence's .22 pistol loaded with snake shot.

Millie loved the seasonal bloom of service berries and dogwood. She had made her first sighting of a pileated woodpecker the day before. It was nearly fifteen inches tall. She had watched him send wood chips flying. Bluebirds were in abundance, as were house finches and purple finches too. She enjoyed the quiet on the river. Raymond was skilled enough to handle the canoe by himself, almost silently, leaving her free to use the binoculars and her copy of a field guide to North American birds.

For Raymond, it was delightful to watch her laughing, making discoveries, and sharing them with him, her hair flashing in the sunlight and her smile as infectious as a small child's. Inside this stunning lady lived a little girl who was brimming over with glee just to be alive. He didn't know which part of her was more beautiful, but he knew that in her presence, he was made whole, and life was worthwhile.

"Here, let me get that," he said, picking the suitcase up with one hand and the cooler with the other.

"Thanks. Are you going to need help taking the canoe off the car roof?" She carried the picnic basket in her arms and managed to balance a pair of sleeping bags on top of it while snagging the screen door with one finger and prying it open.

"Probably, but let's get everything else inside first." He put the suitcase down by the laundry room door and carried the cooler into the kitchen. She dumped the sleeping bags down the basement stairs and joined Raymond at the kitchen counter.

"You were the most beautiful girl on the river today," he said, stepping in close to hold her from behind.

"That's not saying much. There weren't that many girls out today. So watch the flattery, Bub. It's a dead giveaway."

In the distance, they heard a siren.

"Let's get the canoe stowed, and we can clean out the car tomorrow."

They held hands as they stepped down off the porch.

"I'll go open the garage and get the light on. You bring the car in," Millie said.

"Okay." Raymond went around the rear of the new Chevy, headed for the driver's side. He stopped for a moment and listened to more sirens.

A fire truck, lights flashing, sirens wailing, raced up the street toward them. Red lights bounced off the houses. With a roar, it barreled past, the siren's pitch falling as it went, lights retreating and sounds dwindling.

"I wonder what it could be this time of night," Millie said.

"I've counted two cruisers, at least one ambulance, and a couple of fire trucks so far."

"I don't know how you do that," she said. "All sirens sound alike to me."

"It was something we learned when we were kids. We used to claim we could tell who was driving. That part was just bluff, but we got pretty good."

He opened the door and slid into the driver's seat while Millie swung the garage doors open. Raymond had devised a simple system. Two loops of rope hung down from the rafters overhead, with the free ends passing through a pair of pulleys. She guided him in and then slipped one of the ropes underneath the bow and moved it close to the roof rack. He did the same thing with the rear loop. Then he released the tie-downs, and they pulled at the same time to hoist the canoe. He tied off his end, and she tied off hers.

Dusting her hands together, she teased him, "If you were any kind of engineer, you would have mounted both pulleys close enough together that you could do this by yourself."

"Yeah, well if you were any kind of wife, you would have come out here to fix it yourself just to make your point."

"I'll get right on that."

"I wish you would."

As they were closing up the garage, the phone rang in the house. Millie dashed off to answer it while Raymond switched off the light and matched the doors up to shove them closed. As he stepped back into the house, he saw Millie standing in the kitchen doorway with a puzzled look on her face.

"Who was it?"

"I don't know. I didn't get to it in time. But who would call us at midnight?"

"Beats me. Probably a wrong number. If it's important, they'll call back."

"Raymond, something is wrong. All the sirens. No one ever calls us at midnight."

He thought about that. The sirens didn't keep going all the way out to the highway. In fact, by the sound of it, they shut down somewhere in town. Then they heard another one, but it was heading towards them. The siren was getting louder. He heard it top the hill at Main Street. It was definitely coming their way.

"Raymond, what about the shop?"

"Better get a coat and lock up, Millie. This sounds like Bud."

"You're bluffing."

"Not this time."

They couldn't get any closer than half a block away. The heat was too intense. Boiling orange flames spewed black smoke into the night air. Bud found the command post where Fire Chief Pearson Dunklin was directing his firefighters by radio. He worked alongside Police Chief Al Jennings, who was doing the same thing for his men. Bud led Raymond and Millie over to them and caught Chief Dunklin's eye. Dunklin nodded and continued to talk into the radio. "We may not be able to do anything about that now. The roof's caving in, and the walls could go any minute, so keep the men clear. We'll look for gas cans later. Bobbie, the owners just got here, and I need to talk to them. You're fire boss until I get back to you, okay? Right. Good. I'll ask them." He clicked off the mike and turned to Bud, who made quick introductions.

"Dunk, Raymond and Millie Thornton. He owns the building."

"Thanks, Bud. Listen, our guys need to know if you have any volatiles in there and where."

Raymond ran his hands through his hair and thought. "Varnish. We had varnish in the lean-to out back. Turpentine, stuff like that. Lots of wood inside. The shop floor is wood. Trash cans filled with sawdust and scraps."

"No, no. I'm talking about flammable liquids that could explode and shower my guys with fire. Anything like that? Alcohol? Gasoline? Fuel oil? Propane? Acetylene torches? Oxygen tanks? Gas stove? Water heater?"

"Uhm, uhm ... bottle of rubbing alcohol in the bathroom, no welding equipment, no O2, no gas, no diesel. Stove and water heater are natural gas. Meter's in back."

"Give me a second. Bobbie, this is Dunk. Varnish and turpentine in the shed. Negative on the flammables inside except for a bottle of isopropyl in the bathroom. Water heater and stove are natural gas. You have? Good. Okay. More in a second. Stand by."

"Raymond, to your knowledge, could anyone be in there?"

"Tater Gilmore lives there. I don't know if he was home. Do you have reason to believe somebody is in there?" he asked, tapping his nose. He guessed Chief Dunklin would understand the signal. He did. It was not a smell you could forget.

"No. Not so far. Whoever set this used a lot of gas. It's gonna be a total loss. We're trying to limit the damage right now. Cops are getting folks out of the surrounding houses now." He turned to Bud.

"Sheriff, Al's guys are busy with traffic and evac. I need you to do something."

"What?"

"Torches set a fire just to watch. We probably have a firebug out there," he said thumbing toward the crowd of onlookers. "Normal reactions are shock, awe, fear, or fascination. Whoever did this is gonna be proud of his work. Ask your guys to scout the crowd. Look for someone with a smirk, maybe offering to help."

Bud wheeled and left, pulling his radio out of his belt. Millie's knees were growing weak. Raymond was holding her up.

"Why don't you folks have a seat," Dunklin said, sweeping a hand toward the fire engine running board. "Hang around. We're gonna need you."

He raised his walkie-talkie again. "Bobbie? Dunk. One possible victim. Resident's whereabouts are unknown. Yeah, I'm back. I'll take command."

There was a lot going on. The hedges had carried the fire to the neighboring houses. People in bare feet and pajamas were being herded down the street, looking over their shoulders to see what was happening to their homes.

Raymond helped support Millie as she sank down to the running board. He sat beside her, wrapping a protective arm around her shoulder. Raymond looked up to watch the legacy of Clarence Biederman going up in flames.

The wall with the painted sign sagged and pitched out onto the driveway, dumping concrete blocks onto Tater's burning truck. Instead of wailing and weeping, Millie and Raymond held hands, their heads bowed in prayer.

It was just what Brick came to see. He had been looking forward to their misery. *It's too fucking late for that now,* he thought. *You should have done that a long time ago. God's paying you back for what you done to me.* The very next thing he saw was Deputy Sam Whiteside walking his way.

Chapter 28

▼

Nobody's Business

Monday, May 24, 1976, 8:16 AM

Tater rode up in the passenger side of his girlfriend's car. He was dressed in his painter's whites, ready to go to work except for one little problem: His truck. It was canted at an odd angle because the right front tire was nothing but ashes. Blackened and blistered paint greeted him where yesterday it had been sky blue. But in case that wasn't enough, it had been pulverized when the wall fell on it.

He stood looking at an empty black hole in his life that used to be an apartment and a business surrounded by homes. The only signs of life were a fire department van parked at the curb and a sheriff's patrol car.

Two figures knelt inside the remnants of the building, inspecting the charred remains of the bathroom wall outlets. Bud saw Tater and stood to walk over to him.

"Tater, you have no idea what a relief it is to see you."

"Baby," Alyssa said leaning out of her car window, "that ain't your truck, is it?"

"Sheriff Bud, what the hell happened here?" Tater asked as the man approached him.

"Looks like arson. Just for the record, where were you last night about eleven o'clock?"

Tater stared at the building and waved a hand absent-mindedly toward Alyssa's car.

"I was over at her place."

"Baby, don't go telling stuff like that. It ain't nobody's business but ours."

"That's not quite accurate, ma'am," Bud said bending down to look at her as he removed his hat to wipe his brow. "It's a police matter. If Tater was with you, it would be good to say so now."

"Well, he was."

"All night?"

"Baby, do I have to answer that?"

"Just answer the man's questions, Alyssa. Or come see me in jail."

"Well, yes. He was with me all night, but he slept on the couch!"

"So you wouldn't know if he slipped out, say about ten thirty and came back later, all smoky and smelling of gasoline?"

"Ain't no way that coulda happened."

"Why is that?"

"Because he couldn't have done that without me knowing it."

"Because he didn't sleep on the couch?"

Silence.

"Look, ma'am, you are both grown-ups. It's none of my business what your relationship is. But it would sure help us find out who did this by eliminating those who didn't have an opportunity. That's all I really need to know."

"No lie?"

"No lie."

Alyssa smiled bashfully.

"I can assure you, Sheriff, that man standing right over there didn't have no chance to get outta my sight last night—anytime. He was with me the whole night."

"Thank you, ma'am. Thank you. And if I might add, he's one lucky guy—on several counts." Bud smiled as he put on his hat. He was pretty sure he had just seen her blush.

He walked over to Tater and patted his arm.

"Looks like you're gonna need a new truck, pal."

"Bud, I shoulda been here. This is all my fault."

"Now how do you figure that?"

"If I'da been here, this wouldn't have happened."

"Either that, or we could have been trying to fish you out of these ashes just now." He glanced over at Alyssa and back. "I'd say you made an excellent choice."

"But what's Raymond gonna say?"

"He's gonna say now you have to get married."

"What?"

"C'mon, Tater, think about it. When Alyssa there figures out she saved your life last night, your roaming days are over. Why, it's nothing short of divine intervention." Bud had that crinkle in the corner of his eye that always gave him away.

Tater cracked a smile and chuckled.

"Can you keep that to yourself awhile? I could use about a three-day head start."

Bud glanced at Alyssa and back. Then he turned toward the gutted building.

"You've got real complications now, Tater. And when Alyssa's done with you, you're still gonna have to answer to God."

Tater burst out laughing, and Bud turned to look.

"What? Do you think I'm joking?"

Tater doubled over. He stared at the ground for a moment and then up at the truck and shook his head. Then he turned to face Bud.

"Guess I'm gonna go see the insurance company. The bank ain't gonna be too happy either. Any idea who did it?"

"Not yet. We picked someone up for questioning, but it is hard to put the match in his hand. All we've got is circumstantial evidence and no witnesses."

"Anybody who'd do this gotta be crazy."

"That's the working theory right now. By the way, I should let you know we tried to search your glove box for the registration to verify ownership. Everything inside is burned to a crisp. Hope your insurance guy has a copy of your policy."

"Damn."

"Yeah. That about says it all right there."

Chapter 29

▼

Raleigh Police Department

Monday, May 24, 1976, 9:52 AM

"Mr. Thornton, how much insurance did you have on your business?" asked Detective Ned Shoemaker.

"It wasn't insured."

"You mean to tell me that you had all that woodworking equipment and didn't have any insurance on it?"

"Yes, that's the situation. I didn't even consider the possibility of a fire."

"How was your business doing? Were you struggling to make ends meet?"

"Business was good. I had ten or twelve jobs lined up over the next two months and a little money in the bank."

"So, I don't get it? Why would you burn down your own business?"

"You really don't get it, do you? I didn't burn down my own business."

"Prove it."

"Listen, Ned, don't jack me around. I don't have any reason to do that. How would I benefit by destroying my own livelihood?"

"I don't know yet. That's what I'm trying to figure out."

"I wasn't born yesterday. You want to know if I had a motive. There isn't one, so let's look at opportunity. Millie and I were on the Jack's Fork River all weekend, camping and floating. We didn't get back to town Sunday night until eleven thirty or so.

"We probably still have receipts for food and gas with dates stamped on them. In fact, why don't you go talk to the Bartletts next door? They may be able to tell you to the minute when we pulled into the driveway. We were still unpacking the car when the fire truck roared by. You can get the call-out time from the fire department."

"You have gas cans in your garage, don't you? Everybody has a gas can."

"Nope. No need. Our yard is so small I cut it with an Armstrong push mower. It's good exercise."

"So if you didn't do it, then who did?"

"You're the detective here. Do your job. Just quit looking for a cheap and easy way to pin this on me."

"I'm trying, but you're gonna have to help me out a bit here. Why would anyone want to burn down your place?"

"Well, let's see. There's plain old business competition. But I can't think of anyone who would do that. Tater Gilmore may have enemies. He was living there. He's black, so it could be some sort of racial thing."

"We're already looking into that. But let me stay focused on you for right now. Did you keep anything of value at the shop unrelated to your business? Art, photos, books, guns, collectibles of any kind that someone would want to steal and cover up?"

"A few books. Paperbacks mostly. The only other thing I can think of is the Donny Weber file."

"The Donny Weber file? What the hell is that?"

"Ask Bud about it. Donny was this thirteen-year-old kid found hanged in a barn in 1959. We were a year or so older. We have tried ever since to figure out who killed him. Kind of a childhood obsession."

"So where was this file, and what was in it?"

"In a box on top of the cabinets in the kitchen. It was mostly newspaper clippings and photos. It had a copy of his death certificate and a rolled-up chart we put together trying to figure out who could have done it."

"Describe this chart."

"It was junior detective stuff, on poster paper. Down one side, we listed all the facts from the papers. Beside it was a column of facts from the death certificate. That told us what we knew for sure and what could be speculation."

"How old were you guys again?"

"Fourteen."

"What made you come up with this?"

"Bud was our detective. He read everything he could get his hands on about investigative techniques. It was his idea."

"Did you, uhm, have any possible suspects?"

"Only one. Purely circumstantial. Brick Donavan. He was picking on Donny when we broke it up. I coldcocked him with a Latin book. He was out to get me after that. He got sent to prison for trying to stomp Larry Gilmore to death. We were playing baseball. Gilmore was sliding into third base."

"What happened?"

"When I saw Brick kicking and stomping on Larry, I charged. He was getting ready to kick him in the head when I tackled him. Hard. Tore up his knee when I did it. He got expelled and did a couple of years in the state pen for aggravated assault. I testified against him."

"Tell me everything you know about Brick Donovan."

Monday, May 24, 1976
The Raleigh Journal-Messenger

Business Burns, Local Man Held for Questioning

By Lou Baxter

Minutes before midnight last night, Lavonia Tuttle was awakened by a bright orange light in her bedroom window at 344 West Fifth Street. When she rose to investigate, she discovered the Biederman and Son Cabinetry shop next door fully engulfed in flames. The business was destroyed and nearby homes damaged.

"Fire was leaping up through the trees, higher than the telephone poles by half," she told this reporter. "I grabbed the phone in the kitchen and called the operator to report it and ran out the back door. My dog Biscuit went to barking earlier, but I made him hush. His hackles were way up. If I had called it in then, this wouldn't have happened."

Fire Chief Pearson Dunklin says several factors point to arson. Apparently, an intruder broke in through a storage area in the back and poured gasoline all around. An empty gas container was found at the scene.

Police officers evacuated nearby residents and controlled traffic while sheriff's deputies looked for persons with suspicious behavior. A local man has been held overnight for questioning. The shop, owned and operated by Raymond "Sonny" Thornton, was destroyed. Investigators report the business was not insured. The county hospital treated four people for smoke inhalation and minor injuries. As of this morning, all of them, including one firefighter, have been released.

Chapter 30

▼

Raleigh High School

Monday, May 24, 1976

Raymond entered by the door nearest the office and went up the wide staircase to the second floor. It was getting close to five o'clock. Despite being distracted by the fire, Millie decided to spend the afternoon taking down posters and returning books to the storage cabinets to protect them from the maintenance men. It was a practice she had adopted early in her career when over the summer, painters not only changed the color of her room, but also anointed books and posters as well.

He knew there would be boxes to store at home until next fall. It was easier than trying to get them unstuck from a freshly refinished floor. There was never enough storage at school. Over the years, he had become accustomed to the cleaning-storing-hauling ritual. He was there to take the last load home.

As he entered her classroom, he heard a radio on the corner of her desk playing Mozart. Millie was nowhere to be seen. The blackboard was spotless except for a slogan. In her handwriting, it said: "Grammar matters. It proves you are educated." It made him smile.

He was adrift in an unfamiliar world now. His had burned to the ground last night, although in some ways, it felt like a week had passed. Not even Bud could offer much help. He was involved primarily as a criminologist, but it was not a sheriff's department case. Some years ago, an interesting question arose while he was trout fishing with Police Chief Al Jennings. Why were the two departments duplicating effort? Why not pool their resources instead? The solution was a memorandum of understanding which worked as long as both sides remembered who had jurisdiction over each case.

Raymond heard Millie coming down the hall before he saw her. Her heels struck a distinctive cadence on the terrazzo floor. It reminded him of a prancing show horse, but he kept that observation to himself. He slipped into a desk in the front row, clamped his legs together, interlaced his fingers, placed his hands on the desk, and sat in his best posture. As Millie entered the room, he pretended to be a model student. She didn't miss a beat.

"Detention again, is it, Mr. Thornton?"

"Yes, ma'am."

"What did you do this time?"

"They said I was playing with matches, but it wasn't me."

"Okay, Raymond. You need to tell me exactly what happened at the police station," she said as she slid into the school desk next to him.

"Well, first of all, I am pretty certain Detective Ned Shoemaker is convinced that I am innocent. I had neither motive nor opportunity. As for means, anyone can buy a can of gas."

"So who did it?"

"Are you sure you want to know?"

"It's not that I want to know. I need to know. Someone committed an act of violence. I no longer have the luxury of ignorance."

"They are looking at Brick Donovan."

"*That* Brick Donovan?"

"Yep."

"Tell me about it."

"Ned wanted to hear everything, all the way back to the Donny Weber story. As I told him about my history with Brick, we played connect-the-dots."

"What do you mean?"

"It only makes sense in looking back on it. Living through it, the picture was always cloudy. Do you want the dots or just the dots?"

"I pretty much know the dots, so connect them for me."

"Okay. First dot: Brick is tormenting Donny. Wally, Bud, and I intervene, and in the process, I whip Brick in front of his gang. Second dot: He pops me with a towel in gym. I return the favor and humiliate him in front of his gang. We go to the principal's office. I get a lecture; he gets detention. Third dot: He picks on me in dodgeball; I coldcock him, and once more, he loses face. Fourth dot: Coach Mertz gets on his case, and a couple of weeks later, the man's car gets torched. Fifth dot: Donovan tries to stomp Larry Gilmore to pieces, and I take him out, shattering his knee in the process. Sixth dot: Donovan is tried and convicted of aggravated assault for what he did to Larry. My testimony sends him to prison for two years."

"That doesn't mean he set the shop on fire."

"No, it doesn't. But in the words of Detective Ned, 'Did it ever occur to you that maybe he don't like you?'"

"Bud said he spotted him in the crowd during the burning at the Weber place. He ran when Bud saw him, as though he was guilty of something. And dot number ... what are we up to now?"

"Seven."

"Dot number seven: My old pal Deputy Whiteside picks him up last night at the fire for 'suspicious behavior,' which is cop talk for smelling like gasoline and acting like a squirrel. He is still in jail."

"No."

"Yes. They suspect him of doing it, but all the evidence is circumstantial. They either have to charge him with a crime or release him. He could be back out on the streets tonight, so watch out for him. Bud figures they will release him and keep an eye on him for a while."

"What will happen then?"

"Do you want to hear what they told me, or what I think?"

"I need to hear both."

"I got a lot of backslapping. 'We'll find whoever did this and put him away. Trust us to do our jobs.'"

"And what do you think?"

Raymond rubbed his eyes with the heels of his hands and thought about the question. He let out a sigh and answered. "They won't charge him. It's too circumstantial. The paint on the gas can burned away, so there aren't any fingerprints to put him at the scene. There seem to be no witnesses."

"But he had a reason and the chance to do it."

"Yes, but that isn't enough. A good defense attorney doesn't have to prove innocence. All he has to do is to introduce a reasonable doubt."

"How?"

"Discredit me as a drunk. Fabricate some reason for me to engage in arson for hire. Identify the hundreds of locals who filled gas cans that weekend. Conjure up some sort of alibi for Brick. Without forensic evidence to put Brick there with a can of gas in one hand and a match in the other, they won't waste the court's time. Brick may not be smart, but he is not dumb enough to confess."

"So a guy who hates you enough to burn down your business is going to be loose in the community again?"

"Millie, I am afraid so. And we have to be careful until he screws up and goes back to jail. It's either that or leave town."

"We're not doing that, are we?"

"No, this is our home. I am not going to run and hide from a goddamned garbage man."

"Raymond? Are you thinking what I think you're thinking?"

"What is that?"

"Are you going to go have one of your 'little chats' with him?"

"Not this time, Millie."

"Why not?"

"Because Ned Shoemaker thinks he may have killed Donny Weber. If he is a murder suspect, you can bet Shoemaker will be watching. I don't need to be picked up standing over Brick with a baseball bat in my hands. I am afraid this time, we have no choice but to wait and watch."

"Where's your .45?"

"In the gun safe in the basement. Why?"

"Because I want you to get it out and show me how to use it. Before this is over, we may need it."

"I can do that, but it may not be enough."

"What do you mean?"

"It takes more than one gun to go to war. You need a gun in the car and one in your purse. We need a shotgun downstairs and a .38 in the nightstand. I carried the .45 in combat so I'll use it. But you must learn how to load and shoot all of them."

"Okay, I will. But I am also going to pray that Brick isn't stupid enough to make us use them."

"Good idea."

Chapter 31

Reconstruction

Saturday, June 12, 1976

Millie and Raymond spent many hours pondering what to do. His advance for *A Soldier's Heart* was invested in stocks and bonds. The royalty checks went into savings and CDs. They chose to live just as they always had to preserve lifelong friendships. They lived on what they earned and put the proceeds from the book aside for retirement. Now that had changed.

"Do you plan to rebuild?" she asked him as they stood in front of the burned-out lot looking at the damaged houses on either side.

"Yeah, I'll reopen the shop somewhere, but not here."

"Tell me what you're thinking."

"This neighborhood has tolerated the noise of my saws and planer long enough. If I were to rebuild right here, every cut would remind them of that night. I think they deserve peace and quiet."

"So you're going to move the shop?"

"I think so. Yes."

"I have an idea."

"What's that?"

"Hire some local contractors to restore those houses. Tater can paint them."

"Well, Millie, they probably have homeowner's insurance."

"Maybe so, but I don't think these folks should have to file a claim, do you? It's not their fault they got damaged. I think it's our responsibility to see them made whole."

"I like that idea. It feels right," Raymond said.

"What should we do with this lot?"

"I'm inclined to get a dozer in here. Make a place to unload materials and park trucks. After that, I just don't know."

"Why not put in a park?"

"That's an interesting idea."

"Instead of an empty lot, leave behind some trees, flowers, a couple of benches, maybe a gazebo. Dedicate it to your dad and to Clarence. What do you think?"

"I like it."

"Okay. Where will you put your shop?"

"There are several businesses going in out by the old drive-in. It's zoned commercial, so I could even close the doors and work at night if I had to."

"Do you need to build a new building?"

"I thought about that, but the old Laundromat isn't doing much business. I was thinking I could buy that place and renovate it. Concrete floors, water, lights, city sewer … more power than I need. All I have to do is to move some outlets. With a sign next to the highway, everyone in town will know we are back in business inside a week."

"What will that cost?"

"A little over half of what it would take to build from scratch. It can be up and running in a few weeks instead of a few months."

"Raymond, I say do it."

"Good. I close on the building next week."

She laughed out loud.

"Thanks for discussing it with me first."

"You're welcome."

As Raymond's plans were coming together, Tater made a clever suggestion.

"Why not turn it into a contest?"

"What are you talking about?"

"Get two teams on those houses, and see which one can finish first and which one does the better job."

"Offer a prize?"

"No, two prizes. One for the first to finish, and one for the best job."

"Explain what you're thinking, Tate."

"Okay. Think like a contestant for a minute. If you won the prize for finishing first and your competitor won the prize for quality, who has the best bragging rights?"

"You are a devious man. Anybody ever told you that?"

"But get this," Tater said with a grin. "If you won *both* prizes, now who has bragging rights? See, I figure a little competition can get this cleaned up, and we can have some fun with it too."

"That is brilliant!"

"Thank you."

The two homes were unequally damaged, so after a great deal of wrangling, the crew with the biggest job was given a four-day head start. The competition agreed when they realized it gave them four days to strategize. What became known as the "Fifth-Street Build-Off" got underway at daybreak on Saturday, June 26, right in the middle of the Well Stone Writing Festival. A crowd gathered by the vacant lot to see the start of the competition. No one anticipated the size of the betting pool at Dutch's Diner or the interest in the *Journal-Messenger's* progress reports.

Jason Niedegerke, one of the contractors, struck up a conversation with his old friend, "Swede" Johansson.

"Swede, I've been giving this contest some thought."

"No foolin'? You that scared?"

"No. But I don't think it is fair for us to take both those prizes away from you."

"All right, Jason. What are you up to now?"

"Well, hell. Everybody is going to come to us for their houses. We will have to turn away business, and that ain't good. And in a strictly theoretical sense, if you were to win, you'd have the same problem."

"So you *are* worried."

"It's not that. I'm just thinking the best outcome for both of us is to have this here contest to end in a tie."

"You trying to rig this thing?"

"Actually, I'm trying to figure out how we can get the best publicity out of the deal."

So the last daub of paint was applied simultaneously by Sonny on one house and by Tater on the other. By the end of July, the scars from the fire were gone. Both houses sparkled. Between them was a little park with a fountain and a gazebo. It had become public knowledge that they only billed Raymond for materials. Business had never been so good. When Tater and Sonny started working out of the new location, there was one major difference. This time, the building was insured.

Friday, July 16, 1976

The summer did not go as well for Brick Donovan. Detective Shoemaker decided that being unable to charge him with arson didn't keep him from putting a squeeze on him. Today, he was going to visit the offices of Petiole Hauling, and he wanted Brick to know he was doing it. At five thirty in the morning, he parked on Bluff Street. When Brick shoved through the rusty chain-link gate, Ned started his engine and turned on his headlights. Brick glanced across the street and got a two-fingered salute from the detective. Driving away from the curb in his old Ford, he watched the rearview mirror. Shoemaker pulled out behind him. The black-and-white stayed with him, even through a coffee stop at the 7-Eleven.

By the time Donovan got to work, he was busy pretending he had not been followed. But with a few furtive glances, he saw Shoemaker park the squad car and enter the unpainted concrete block office. He was sweating now but fought to hide his agitation and clocked in. He swapped lies with the boys and hauled himself up into the truck and pulled out just like he did any other day. Only when he was a half block away and out of sight did he allow himself to pound on the steering wheel and scream and swear.

CHAPTER 32

▼

THE ARROW OF TIME

Friday, July 16, 1976, 5:00 PM

When Brick Donovan pulled back into the lot at five o'clock, the guy at the gate told him Junior Petiole wanted to see him. As he opened the metal door, he noticed it didn't smell much better inside, but at least an oscillating fan in the corner churned the air. Melanie, all three hundred forty-six pounds of her, sat at an old metal desk with no pencil drawer and a file that wouldn't close. The desk was ugly, but it was free—a lot like Melanie.

"Junior said he wants to talk to you," she said popping her gum.

"So I heard. So why don't you prance in there and tell him I'm here."

"Kiss my butt," she said mashing on an intercom button. "Junior, it's Brick. Got your gun?"

"Tell him to get his sorry ass in here."

"Mr. Petiole said he would be happy to see you now, Mr. Donovan," she said as she took another swig of something brown in a yellow cup. Brick ignored her and pushed open the door into Junior's office. Inside, a window air conditioner rumbled noisily in an effort to beat back the heat.

"What's happening?"

"Cop says you burned down the cabinet shop. That right?"

"If I did, I'd be in jail now, wouldn't I? I go see what all the commotion is about and a deputy decides I look guilty. Only thing is, see, they got a problem. They ain't got no evidence, some little shit like that."

"He said you been tryin' to nail Sonny Thornton since high school. What's the deal?"

"He's the prick who got me thrown out of school and fucked up my knee. Then he testified against me so I get sent up for a coupla years. I figure he's got something coming."

"Well, answer me this. Did you whack some kid named Donny Weber?"

"What? ... What the hell you talkin' about? You better back up here, Junior, and take it real slow, 'cause I'm about to get pissed off."

"You do that, and you get fired; do you understand me? Now sit down and shut up."

Brick looked around and spotted an empty orange bucket chair someone had thrown away years ago. He sat down. Blood vessels popped out on his neck and forehead. His face turned purple, and the corners of his mouth twisted into a scowl.

"Don't ever threaten me, Junior. Not you or anybody else."

Without a word, Junior opened the drawer on his right, pulled out a .44 Magnum, and thumped it down hard on the desk. His eyebrows twisted into knots, and the fierceness in his face made Brick swallow hard.

"Save the goddamned hate face for somebody who cares, you sorry sack of shit, and listen real nice to what I am saying to you. Some of the things we got going on here, we don't need no cops snooping around. Do I make myself clear?"

"Yeah."

"I don't give a rat's ass about you and Thornton and your miserable life. I don't give a damn about some dead kid. That's all in the past. I can't do nothing about it. But there is some shit happening right here right now, that if it gets on you, it ain't never gonna come off. 'Cause I am the guy carrying the bucket. Do you hear what I'm saying to you?"

"I hear ya, but I don't know what you want me to do."

"I'm gonna say this plain enough so you can understand. Pack your shit and get out. You're fired."

"Aw, hell, Junior. C'mon! What am I supposed to do? I show up on time, and I work hard, and I do my job, and I don't cause nobody no trouble."

"Stop right there," Junior said picking up the gun and waving it at the wall. "This ain't no open forum. It ain't subject to debate. We took all day to think this through, Dad and me, and it's not like we got a choice. So get your stuff and get outta here, and don't never come back, not even for Melanie. Now get out."

Brick stood and gestured palms up. "But how am I gonna eat? Come on, Junior, give me a break here."

Junior eased the hammer back with his thumb slowly so that Brick could hear both clicks. Just as slowly, he leveled the barrel at Brick's heart.

"I been trying, asshole. I'm letting you walk outta here. But if that's not what you want, there is another way."

Brick raised both hands and backed away. He felt a burning sensation at the point on his chest where the gun was aimed. As he turned, the aim point drifted across his side and onto his back. It felt like a laser searing his flesh. He tore through the door and ran for his truck. He vanished out the front door before Melanie could hurl an insult at him. Through the barred window, she saw his truck pull out, spraying everything behind it with gravel and dust.

Moments later, Junior came out of his office with his coat over his shoulder. Melanie's mouth hung open in mid-chew as she turned to look at him.

"What are you starin' at? Day's over. Time to go home," he said. "Lock up on your way out."

Melanie was trying to make sense out of what she just heard. As the door slowly closed behind her boss, she took her meaty arm off the yellow tablet filled with handwriting. The last sentence was incomplete: "I been trying, asshole. I'm letting you walk out of h—"

She waited until the green Lincoln Continental had left the parking lot before she finished transcribing what she had heard. When she was done, she reread it and made a few corrections. It might not be exactly word for word, but there was no mistaking the gist of it. When she finished, she picked up the phone.

Later that night

The note stuck in the front door from Bud was cryptic and brief. Betty Ann checked the back side of the paper to see if there was anything else. There wasn't. She went straight to the phone and called Wally at the store.

"Hey, hot stuff. We may have to change our plans for tomorrow night."

"How come?"

"Bud left a note in the door. It sounds important."

"What's it say?"

"It says, 'It's about Donny. We have to talk, and it can't wait. My cabin, Saturday evening at six. I'll grill. Get a babysitter. I'll pay. Beau.' Why sign it 'Beau'?"

"Would you sign a note B.O.?"

"Guess not."

"That's it? That's all he said?"

"That's it."

"Can we drop the kids over at Mom and Dad's to spend the night?"

"Probably. Do you want me to call?"

"Would you?"

"Okay. But what do I tell them? I can't say that Bud called an emergency meeting of the Three Musketeers."

"Sure you can. My folks would understand that as quick as anything else. Tell them Bud thought it was urgent."

"What if they have other plans?"

"Tell them what Bud said. They will change their plans. He has a whole lot more pull with my folks than I do … But just in case they can't, do we have a plan B?"

"I could call Lizabeth down the street. The kids think she's cool."

"Okay. Let me get the shelf stocking started, and I'll be home as soon as I can."

"Okay."

"Betty Ann?"

"Yeah, babe?"

"Don't be scared. Bud always knows what he's doing."

"Okay. Love you."

"Love you too."

Until that moment, it never occurred to Betty Ann to be scared.

Bud was pretty sure he knew where to find Raymond. He drove past the old drive-in. The lights were on in the Laundromat, and two pickups were parked out front. He pulled in next to them and made his way around a bin piled with broken drywall and construction debris. When he got to the front window, he realized the glass was gone. Right on the other side of it, Sonny and Tater were tearing out a half wall that once provided electrical and plumbing connections between two rows of washing machines.

"Hey, excuse me, kids. Can I get a couple of hot dogs and a big orange to go?"

"See, Tater? Just like I told you? Whenever real work is going on, some jackass will walk up and say, 'Hi, guys, whatcha doin'?'"

"Don't sell him nothin' boss. He'll bust us for running an unlicensed kitchen."

Bud's expression turned serious.

"This is not exactly a social call here, boys. I got word today that Brick Donovan may be going on the warpath. I'm glad you're here, Tater, because this involves you too."

Raymond and Tater exchanged glances and walked over to the window to hear what Bud had to say. Tater folded his powerful arms and leaned against the window ledge. Raymond mopped his face with a red bandana and waited for Bud to explain.

Across the highway, behind a clump of cedars in a fencerow, Brick Donovan lowered the crosshairs of his deer rifle from Raymond's head and quietly withdrew to the safety of his truck. He ejected the single cartridge from the chamber before hanging the rifle in the rear window. He watched the men across the street. They were talking so intently they didn't look over at him when he started the engine. He pulled on his lights and eased out onto the highway just like any average guy going about his business.

Chapter 33

The Cabin

Saturday, August 14, 1976

Bud waited until they were all there before he put the steaks on the grill. The charcoal was ready. He had a big bowl of tossed salad on the table and ears of corn in a pan of water on the stove. On the deck, a big cooler he had hauled in from town held iced beer and soda. His culinary skills showed a side of him the ladies had never seen.

"What can we do to help?" Betty Ann asked.

"I started the corn about five minutes ago. If you don't mind, could you keep an eye on it for me? If we get this right, the steaks and the roasting ears should be done at about the same time." He got everyone's order, tossed the steaks on the grill, and glanced at his watch.

"Why are you checking the time, Bud? Do you have an appointment?" Wally asked.

"So I can get the steaks right. How do you do it?"

"I use a fork and a meat thermometer," Wally replied.

"That's great if you happen to be standing there at the right time. Get distracted, and you can burn it up or dry it out."

"Okay. So what's your technique?" Tater asked.

"I use the darkroom method."

"What the heck are you talking about?"

"It's like developing prints. Raymond, can you explain it to him?"

"Tater, I'm not sure I know where Bud is going with this, but two things control how dark an image gets when you print it: intensity of the light and length of exposure. You can fudge around a little with the exposure on one end and how long you leave it in the developer on the other, but if the basic exposure is off, it will be hard to salvage."

"What the hell does that have to do with dinner?" Wally asked.

"I'm not grilling steaks here, Wally. I'm printing pictures. There are two basic variables to cooking. How hot is the fire, and how long do I leave the steaks on?"

"Yeah, but you got orders ranging from well done to rare. So how do you get them right?" Tater asked.

"Well, one way is to poke around on six pieces of meat randomly for ten to fifteen minutes. The other is to have a cooking plan."

"A what?" Tater asked.

"That's right. You ordered yours well done, right?"

"Yeah."

"Okay. That steak right there in the middle is yours. It is also the 'control.' This way, they all get done at the same time."

"You gotta be kidding."

"No, he's not, Tater. I see his plan now. Yours is in the hot spot. The four around it are mediums, and this one over here is rare."

"Yeah, but what if somebody wants medium rare or medium well done?"

Bud grinned. "That's the beauty of it, Tater. Not all of these mediums are going to turn out exactly alike, so I compare, and give the pinkest one to the person who ordered medium rare, and the darkest to the one who ordered medium well."

"Oh, man, I got it now," Wally said. "Everyone gets just exactly what they ordered."

"It's all relative, but everybody wonders 'How did he do that?'" Raymond finished.

Tater doubled over laughing and did a little dance. When he finished, he asked, "Man, is everything you do a science?"

Bud thought that over for a moment.

"Pretty much."

When Bud pulled the steaks off the grill, the ladies pulled out the roasting ears. Everyone got a fresh drink and found a place on the deck to eat. Then Bud explained the reason for the gathering.

"What I have to tell you is confidential police information. I could get canned for telling you, but you folks need to know about two things: what's going on with Brick Donovan and something I have learned about how Donny Weber died. But before we get into all that, let's enjoy our meal."

The steaks were just right. The corn on the cob was perfect for melting butter. The tossed salad had lots of tomatoes mixed in with the greens and a generous handful of raisins to give it that zing. The murmur of conversations punctuated with laughter lasted for nearly a half hour until everyone was satisfied. The time had come for business. The night sounds, rich with the serenade of tree frogs and the wistful call of a whippoorwill, enfolded them.

"Okay, folks, listen up. Here goes. Ned Shoemaker is the detective for the Raleigh PD. He got the arson case for the cabinet shop. Raymond told him about keeping files at the shop on the Donny Weber case. He was the kid found hanged in a barn near town back in '59."

"I didn't know nothing about no files," Tater said.

"I know, Tater, but let me continue. Everyone here knows different parts of the story. That means I have to go through it systematically. Let me finish, and then we can answer questions, okay?"

"Sure. I'm sorry."

"No, no, you didn't do anything wrong. I just need to brief everyone to make sure we all have the same information. Everybody understand?"

So in the darkness, on a deck overlooking Lake Osage, Bud quietly led them through the events between Brick Donovan tormenting Donny Weber and the phone call he got the day before.

"So here's what worries me," Bud said leaning forward with his elbows on his knees. "We figure Brick torched Coach Mertz's car and burned down the shop. He has a history of violence and has done time because of it. We know that life inside wasn't easy for him. The word is that he was gang-raped inside and hurt some people to get even. He didn't get extra time for it, mostly because the warden figured they had it coming."

He sat upright and took a deep breath. "So now, not only is Shoemaker looking at Brick for the murder of Donny Weber, he is also pushing the homosexual angle. We know that Brick Donovan goes ballistic whenever anyone accuses him of being queer. So now he is under investigation for a sex-murder of a kid, and he has been fired. That not only makes him desperate, it makes him extremely dangerous."

"So what does that mean for us?" Betty Ann asked, with a tremor in her voice.

"It means that because Wally and Raymond and I have been in this thing since the get-go, we have to watch our backs. In fact, it would be a good idea, Betty Ann, if you and the kids could go away for a while, until we can find him and get him under control."

"You saying you don't know where he is?"

"I'm afraid not. Ray and Millie have a small arsenal, and you folks may need to think about your safety too."

"How'd you know about that?" Millie asked. "Did Raymond tell you?"

"No, Millie, he didn't. I am the sheriff, so I know all the gun dealers in the county. Let's just say they tell me about things that stand out to them. You and Raymond have not done anything wrong. In fact, you did it before I had a chance to suggest it. Credit that to the old warhorse over there."

Raymond had slumped so far down in his chair that his body resembled a reclining board supported at three points: heels, butt, and shoulders. He steepled his fingertips then gently tapped his upper lip with joined fingers. Others may not have read it the way Bud did, but to him, it appeared that Raymond was deciding how to kill Brick Donovan.

"Do you think he might come after me?" Tater asked.

"Let's be clear about this. The person Brick wants to hurt most is Raymond. But he is afraid of him, so he will settle for hurting anyone important to Raymond. That puts a target on each one of our backs. So if you are asking if you should have a gun, I'd say the answer is yes. The most dangerous thing about Brick is that he won't meet you face to face. He's the kind of guy who will take potshots at you from a ditch or try to sneak up on you."

"And as far as he is concerned," Raymond added, "setting a fire is just as good as a gun. Maybe even better, because he can be long gone."

"Now you know why I wanted to explain this with everybody here."

They sat in silence while the night sounds swirled around them.

"Was that the good news or the bad news?" Wally asked to ease the tension.

"Now for the bad news," Bud replied, earning a chorus of groans.

"Well, I can hardly wait," said Betty Ann. "What could possibly be worse than that?"

"This. I am about ninety percent sure Brick had absolutely nothing to do with Donny's death. In fact, Donny may not be a murder victim at all."

Wally went over to the cooler to get another beer. He checked the crowd and handed fresh ones to all those who asked. When he finished, he sat back down.

"Okay. We need to hear what you have to say, but I am pretty sure our enthusiasm is sagging. So can you give it to us in as painless a way as possible?"

"You know, that's a pretty good suggestion," Bud said. "Normally, I'd go through all the things we know for certain to flush out the stuff we don't. But let me tell you the new information I have, and we can see how it fits."

Sighs of relief could be heard in the darkness. Deck furniture creaked while people shifted positions. The moon was up, and an owl hooted in the distance.

"I recently read a study about a secret sex game that kills hundreds of teenagers in the U.S., mostly boys, every year. It's called AEA, for autoerotic asphyxiation. It remains a secret killer for the same reasons it will be difficult for us to talk about, especially in mixed company. It just so happens that the only effective antidote is education and frank discussion. Sonny, natural causes aside, what were the choices for cause of death?"

"Accident, homicide, and suicide," Raymond answered.

"Are those the only choices?"

"On the death certificate?"

"No, not on paper, in real life. In God's whole put-together, can mankind only come up with three alternatives?"

"What are you getting at?" Millie asked.

"Could it be possible for someone to accidentally commit suicide?"

"I'm not sure I'm with you on this, either," Tater said.

"Okay. Here is an example. One guy, call him John Doe, gets so depressed that he gets a gun and commits suicide. The next guy, let's call him Jim Doe, is clowning around with a gun he thinks is empty. He looks in the mirror, puts the gun to his head, makes a funny face, and squeezes the trigger. Only this time, there is a round in the chamber. So what's the difference between these two guys, besides IQ?"

A few chuckled, but no one spoke. Finally, Millie answered. "Intent."

"Exactly."

"Raymond, where on the death certificate is there a check box for intent?"

"It's not there."

"Okay. So did our clown commit suicide, or was he an accident victim? Both these guys died in exactly the same way. They stand in front of a mirror, put a gun to their heads, and squeeze the trigger. Both died at their own hand; one was deliberate, the other an accident. So how do you record it on a form with only three choices?"

"Wow! I see what you are getting at," Wally said. "So how does this apply to Donny Weber?"

"Thanks for asking. Let's go back to Jimmy. His family comes in and finds him. They know him well enough to guess that he died screwing around. They don't want the world to laugh at him for being stupid, so what do they do?"

After a silence, Tater speaks. "They mess around with stuff to make it look like a homicide."

"You're right. That's one of the two possible choices. What's the other?"

"Suicide," Betty Ann said.

"So, with very little time to fix the scene, what do you do? Which is easier to pull off, making it look like a suicide or a homicide? If you fake a murder, you have to manufacture a murderer. If you fake a suicide, you have to manufacture a reason. Come on. The clock is ticking. What are you going to do?"

"In this case," Millie said, "it would be easier to write a phony suicide note. But in Donny Weber's case, it would be easier to fake a murder."

"Absolutely brilliant! You got it exactly right!"

"Wait, wait, wait! I don't get that from what you have told us so far," said Raymond.

"Neither did Millie. She used her imagination to see the truth. I didn't have to tell her all of it."

"Then, for the sake of the rest of us, please fill us in."

"Okay. Here is the pattern for death by AEA. Nine out of ten are boys between the ages of twelve and eighteen—Bright kids, adventurous, inquisitive minds. They learn one way or another that strangulation heightens their sexual arousal and intensifies an orgasm. How do they hear about it? Maybe other kids tell them, or they read about executions by hanging that leave dead men with erections, and they get curious. So they experiment. What they usually don't know is how close to death they are dancing. A choke hold on a person renders them unconscious in less than a minute and dead within two."

"Oh, my god. That's horrifying," Betty Ann said.

"Yes, Betty Ann, it is. Do you see why parents need to talk about it with their kids in order to explain the dangers?"

"Here are some more pieces to the puzzle. Practitioners of AEA devise fail-safe devices: a slipknot they can free, something they can stand on like a hay bale, or some way to release the rope at the other end. If the escape mechanism fails, they die. And since they don't want to walk around with rope burns on their neck, they use a garment or a towel or something to protect themselves from abrasions and bruising.

"Often, there is pornography around, unless a family member destroys it. But the biggest fear for the families is the stigma. They almost always tamper with the scene, especially parents of a young kid. They get rid of the girly magazines, make a choice, and fake the evidence."

"Aw, hell," Raymond said. "Old Man Weber wraps a loop of rope around Donny's wrist and says his hands were tied when he cut him down. And that explains why there were no marks on Donny's wrists."

"The Boy Scout kerchief was used to prevent the marks," Wally added. "That's why the old man and the older brother … What's his name?"

"Dillon."

"That's why they contradicted each other. The old man says he knew for a fact it wasn't Donny's, yet Dillon says he personally gave it to Donny. It was a like they were tossing a rattlesnake back and forth."

"Exactly," Bud said. "But here's the part that really hurts. Having decided to fake a murder, now the old man needs to find a killer. Three fourteen-year-old boys buy into his phony murder story. Why? Because they know Donny Weber was a good kid, and they are too innocent to see anything else. So what's Mr. Weber do? He gets them to promise to find the killer. Then he leaves town."

A breeze stirs the night air, and they reflected in silence on what they had just heard. Wally spoke first.

"I guess we found him."

"Yep. We sure did," said Raymond.

"So here's the question of the night. Who, in all of this, told the truth?" asked Millie. "Certainly not the Webers. Sheriff 'Turnip' and Warren McHenry must have figured it out, but they concealed it by typing in 'Open Verdict' to spare the family."

Bud spoke up. "Somewhere is a state trooper who knows the specimen he took to the lab is semen. But it just wasn't his case."

"Oh, shit," Raymond said. "I wrote an article in the paper that ruined the reputations and careers of those two men."

"At my urging, I have to add," said Millie.

"Yeah, but I exposed them as incompetents."

"I have given that some thought," Bud added. "We thought they were technically incompetent, and, in a way, they were. They should have seen through Weber's deceit. But more importantly, they were ethically lacking. They could have called this senseless death what it was and warned others of the dangers, but instead, they did what everyone else does. Out of misguided sympathy for the family, they buried the truth. And that, ladies and gentlemen, is how AEA survives."

"Listen here, now, Sonny," said Tater. "I got one thing to say, and for that matter, to all you all. If my cousin Larry was here right now, he'd be damned proud of you. I know I am."

It was easier to cry in the dark.

Chapter 34

The Vigil

Sunday, August 15, 1976

It was just something Raymond figured he had to do. That was why his first stop was at a ramshackle old farmhouse located on the tortured terrain that lay beyond the reach of the glaciations in the state. Where he was now, it was all hills and gullies leading down the broad, flat expanse of river basin. That was the only reason Randy "Turnip" Turner raised hogs. Given the land he owned, he had no choice.

Raymond expected to see the robust man of his youth. Before him stood a frail old man who seemed to be shriveling before his eyes. He leaned on a walker wearing Oshkosh coveralls and a filthy white undershirt. But what hurt most was to see his purplish bare feet with gnarled yellow toenails and at least a week's filth on them.

"Sheriff Turner, my name is Raymond Thornton. I have come to apologize to you, sir."

"You what?"

"I have come to apologize for something I did a long, long time ago."

"The name rings a bell, but I don't rightly place your face."

"I was fourteen when we last saw each other. It was about Donny Weber."

Turner's face immediately clouded over. Chewing tobacco trickled down the creases at the corner of his mouth, and his eyes became hard as flint. "I remember who you are now. Boy hero."

Raymond winced.

"You were a pal of that kid who is sheriff now. What's his name?"

"Bud Oswald."

"Yeah, him. Well, kid, I gotta tell you those were the worst years of my life. I can't stand too long. Can we go sit down over there?" He motioned with his head toward a kitchen chair on the corner of the porch.

"Of course. Do you need any help?"

"Darned right I do. But the question is 'Will I accept it?' and the answer's no. Just like it's been all my life."

Raymond reached behind his back and shoved both hands inside his belt to keep from reaching out. He followed patiently alongside the old man as he made his torturous way across the porch.

"The doctor says I got the diabetes and the way I'm living, I ain't gonna last long. I told him it's been too damn long already." He turned around and fell into the chair.

"Ahhhh. All right now. What is it you came out here to say?"

"I know what you and Warren McHenry did."

"About what?"

"Donny Weber's death."

"Look, I'm wearing out fast. I don't have time to decipher no code. So say what you have to say or let me go lay down."

"Donny Weber was playing a sex game by strangling himself while masturbating. Something went horribly wrong, and he killed himself by accident. Mr. Weber found him, cut him down, and figured it out. He got rid of the *Playboy* magazines, or whatever it was, tied a hank of rope around one of Donny's wrists, and called the police. You and McHenry figured it out and took pity on the family. That's why McHenry's inquest ruled 'Open Verdict' and the family left town. How am I doing?"

Tears welled up in the old man's eyes, and his mouth started making a chewing motion. Eventually, he collected himself and choked out what he wanted to say.

"I can die now. The real truth has finally come out. I been scared to meet my maker carrying all that."

"I'm afraid I wrote the article in the paper that caused both of you to lose your jobs."

"From what I recall, that article spoke well of us. Don't seem to me you got anything to apologize for."

This time, the tears were Raymond's. With a sudden chill, he realized the old man completely missed the duplicity of the article. It was too late to explain now. Raymond decided to leave him with a good memory, even if it was false.

"What you and McHenry did was a noble thing. You spared the Webers undeserved torment and bore the brunt of criticism yourself. I have come out here to apologize for writing that article and to tell you that I admire the choices you made. I only regret that Mr. McHenry isn't alive so I can tell him."

"It's all right, sonny. I'll tell him myself. Damn soon, I hope."

Monday, September 13, 1976

"I can't tell him. It's his investigation. You're going to have to do it."

Raymond let out a big sigh, but he knew Bud was right. So he picked up the phone and called the police department.

"Detective Shoemaker, please."

"Shoemaker here."

"Detective, this is Raymond Thornton. Brick Donovan did not kill Donny Weber. I need to come in and tell you about a conversation I had with Sheriff Turner yesterday. Brick scares the crap out of me and my friends, and we need to have you call the dogs off now before he hurts somebody."

"Tell me, Sonny, why should I believe you? How do I know you aren't scared of Donovan and making something up to save your own hide?"

"Two things, you stupid flatfoot: a Bronze Star and a Silver Star. You want a couple of Purple Hearts thrown in too? Where were you during Nam, asshole? For once in your goddamned life, will you shut up and listen to someone else? Go find Sheriff Oswald and ask him to show you a study he found on autoerotic asphyxiation. Then look at the facts in the Weber case. Even a cretin like you can put this puzzle together. When you are done doing your homework, give me a call. Only then will I tell you what Sheriff Turner had to say yesterday." He slammed the phone down.

"That went very well, didn't it?" Bud said.

"Yeah. Just like you said—nice and easy."

Wednesday, September 15, 1976

Ned Shoemaker slipped into the booth at Dutch's Diner across from Raymond.

"What're you having, Sonny?"

Raymond looked up, surprised to see him.

"I'm thinking about the club sandwich and a bowl of tomato soup. Have you had lunch?"

"No. I believe I'll order a bowl of chili and a bottle of catsup. Save room for pie and coffee later on."

Dutch himself came over.

"What'll it be, gents?"

They gave Dutch their orders, and he wandered away without writing any of it down.

"Any chance we'll get what we ordered?"

"He usually gets close enough."

Dutch came back with two cups of coffee well sloshed into the saucer. Shoemaker watched Raymond pull out a bunch of napkins to place between the cup and saucer and soon saw the wisdom of it. He did the same.

"Sonny, I'm not much good at this hat-in-hand stuff, so you're gonna have to help me out here. I did what you said, and I see what you're saying. I'm afraid it makes too much sense for me to ignore. So tell me about your talk with the Turnip."

"He's old and near death, and from what I can tell, he's ready to go. I went out to apologize for writing the article that caused him to lose the election. He thought the article was favorable and didn't see the double meaning in it."

"This is all very touching, but what did he say about the boy's death?"

As dishes clanked around them, Raymond gave the detective a chronological account of the visit to old man Turner's porch. Dutch came out and without a word, put their orders in front of them. It was what Dutch did when he thought important stuff was under discussion. He also knew how to listen.

"I suppose after almost twenty years, we can close that case."

"As what? Accident, homicide, or suicide?"

"Sonny, it sounds accidental to me. What do you think?"

"I think there is hope for you yet."

"I still like Donovan for the arson. Given your history and his, it seems the most logical choice."

"So what do we do to rein him in?"

"Knowing Brick, sooner or later, he's gonna do something stupid, and we'll get him off the street."

Raymond put down his cup and looked at Shoemaker with alarm.

"That's it? That's your plan?"

"You got a better one?"

Raymond took a deep breath and let out a sigh.

"No. But I have to tell you he is apt to wind up dead."

"What do you mean?"

"If he comes after Millie or me, I'll kill him. Same for the Graysons or Bud or Tater. None of us is going to be caught napping. When he turns up dead on the courthouse lawn, you are going to know who set it off. I kinda think you might want to get the bobcat back in the gunnysack."

"Listen, Raymond, I know how you feel. But if you hunt him down and kill him, it is premeditated murder. There is no one in the world who can protect you from that ... not even Bud."

Raymond picked up his fork and jabbed it in Shoemaker's direction.

"You and I gotta get two things straight, Ned. I have never used Bud for protection. He wouldn't hold still for it. You remember my ride home from Emporia chained to a motorcycle?"

"Yeah, I heard about that."

"Well, if that is your idea of preferential treatment, I don't want to know what your notion of persecution is."

"Okay. So what's the second thing we gotta get straight?"

"If I was planning to hunt Brick Donovan down to kill him, he'd have ridden into town across the hood of my truck weeks ago. But if he comes looking for trouble with me and my friends, he is up against a guy who knows how to use deadly force, and it will be the cleanest case of self-defense you have ever seen."

Shoemaker swallowed hard when he looked into Raymond's eyes. He had never heard the expression "killer eyes," but he sure recognized them when he saw them. He held both hands up, palms out, as though he was shoving someone back.

"Raymond, I'll do what I can. I just don't know if I can get the genie back in the bottle."

"If you can't, I can. Just don't come around second-guessing afterwards."

Chapter 35

An Untimely End

Thursday, September 30, 1976

It was Millie's favorite time of year. The heat of summer was gone, and the leaves were about to turn. She loved Indian summer, hot apple cider, football games, and long moonlit nights in the porch swing with Raymond. What she didn't like was being home with the first cold of the school year. But she had no choice. Her whole body hurt, and her sinus headache was unbearable. The antihistamines required for the congestion rendered her goofy, so there it was.

She knew the sequence; first, the sinus congestion, then the post-nasal drip, then the sore throat and bronchitis. Two years ago, she had been hospitalized with pneumonia after such an episode, and she learned her lesson. So, despite the beauty of the morning, she drank the medicine that she knew would knock her out and went upstairs to bed.

Raymond and Tater had the shop sorted out, and Raymond was installing the first set of cabinets he had built since the fire in May. The customers in Claremont had waited patiently to remodel their kitchen after they heard about the fire.

"We've lived with it like this for a long time, so what's a couple of months in the great scheme of things?"

Raymond wanted to get started again on the right foot, so he had put in a lot of extra time making sure he delivered a product Clarence would claim as his own. He was really looking forward to this installation. Tater helped him load the bases and countertop in the truck and headed out to a house-painting job on the north end of town. It was going to be a great day to be outside painting. That all changed as he idled down main street two blocks from his job. A battered old blue Ford pickup pulled up alongside him on the one-way street, but instead of passing, it kept pace with him. He glanced over to see what was going on.

He couldn't place the bearded face grinning at him. Then he spotted a double-barrel shotgun resting across the passenger windowsill. It was aimed right at him. He recognized Brick's eyes at the instant both muzzles flashed, and the world exploded around him. Everything went dark.

It was not long afterward that four sticks of dynamite tossed under Sheriff Oswald's pickup propelled it thirty feet into the air and shattered every window in a five-block radius. Bud was in his office, but he, like everyone else in the building, was peppered with flying glass. By the time he staggered out front to see what had just happened, he was covered in blood from his chest up.

Lucy, despite her own injuries, got on the phone to the hospital and told them what happened. Her ears were still ringing, and she was shouting.

"Send every ambulance you've got to the sheriff's office. We just had a bomb go off down here. Multiple injuries, dozens if not more."

"We only have two available. One is answering a shooting call on Main Street."

"Jesus Christ! What is going on around here? Well, tell the hospital staff this is the disaster we drilled for. Excuse me. I have to go vomit."

Detective Shoemaker was fifteen miles out of town, on his way back from a doctor's appointment in Claremont. He was lost in thought about what the specialist had told him about his enlarged prostate. It took a couple of minutes for what he was hearing on the radio to sink in. *What the hell? A bomb at the sheriff's office? A shooting on Main Street?*

Something clicked into place, and he pulled the microphone out of the holder on the dash and called in.

"Romeo two-six, Dispatch, stand by."

He mashed the gas pedal to the floor and accelerated to seventy in a forty-five-mile-per-hour zone. Worried now, he keyed the mike and yelled back.

"Romeo two-six, negative. Repeat negative. I will not stand by! This is Lieutenant Shoemaker, and I will not stand by. I need to know the name of the shooting victim on Main Street. Now!"

"Romeo two-six, Dispatch, we have not yet had a report on the condition of the shooting victim. Stand by for that information."

"Goddamn it, Edith! Get your head out of your ass and listen to what I am saying! I am not asking about the condition of the victim! I need to know the name, and I mean right now! So take a second and get me the name, all right?"

He reached over and switched on the siren and lights while accelerating down Highway 19 toward the drive-in, clutching the microphone in his hand.

"Romeo two-six, Dispatch."

"Dispatch, Romeo two-six, go ahead."

"The shooting victim has been identified as one Lucius Gilmore, age twenty-nine. Black male. A local painting contractor."

"Jesus Christ, Edith! Is his nickname Tater?"

"Aw, come on, Ned. How in the hell am I supposed to know that?"

"Ask, damn it, ask!"

"Stand by. Sorry. I'll be right back."

The old Laundromat was in view. He didn't see any trucks parked out front. Shoemaker braked hard and skidded into the lot raising a cloud of dust. Just as he got stopped and threw the door open, the radio crackled.

"Romeo two-six, Dispatch. That's affirmative. Victim is Lucius 'Tater' Gilmore."

"Dispatch, I am at the old Laundromat on 19 out near the drive-in, Sonny Thornton's new cabinet shop. He's not here. Send a unit out to Millie and Raymond Thornton's residence on East Tenth."

"Ned, everybody's tied up with the bombing downtown. How far away are you?"

"Five minutes tops. Lights and sound, high speed. Get me some backup, NOW! Suspect's name is Brick Donovan, for the shooting on Main, the bombing, and God knows what else."

As he sailed into town swerving from side to side to avoid traffic, he saw something rising into the sky that made the hair stand up on the back of his neck—smoke!

The printing plant flashed by on his right as he picked up the microphone and called in a fire that seemed to be very near the city park on Tenth Street.

"I'm still four blocks away, but get the fire trucks rolling toward Civic Park, and I'll have an exact address in one minute."

Edith sat at the console holding her breath. She knew what was coming.

"Aw, shit, Edith! It's the Thornton place. Nine-one-four East Tenth. Both floors fully engulfed. It's a total ... shots fired! Repeat, shot's fired ... Aw, Christ ... Somebody's on fire ..."

"Romeo two-six? Romeo two-six, Dispatch. Come in. Romeo two-six ..."

September 16, 1976
Raleigh Journal-Messenger

Local Man Leaves Trail of Death, Mayhem

3 dead, 21 hurt

By Lou Baxter, Editor

It will take many years for Raleigh to get over what took place here yesterday. Our community lost three citizens in what seems to be a homicide, an act of arson, and a shooting in self-defense. Dead are Mrs. Margaret Millicent (McKenna) Thornton, age 43, a beloved high school English teacher, Lucius "Tater" Gilmore, age 29, a local businessman and close personal friend of Mr. and Mrs. Raymond "Sonny" Thornton, and the man thought responsible for their deaths and injuring twenty-one others with an explosive device, Byron "Brick" Donavan, age 34.

A joint task force made up of the Raleigh Police Department, the Raleigh County Sheriff's Department, and the State Highway Patrol has reconstructed the chronology of events using recordings from radio and telephone calls to and from dispatchers for the local police department, sheriff's department, hospital, fire, and ambulance districts.

The events are as follows:

9:21 AM	Police dispatchers received a call of gunshots in the eight hundred block of Main Street and a one-car accident involving a pickup truck striking a porch at 715 Main. Gunshot victim, Mr. Gilmore, pronounced dead at the scene.
9:27 AM	Explosion in the parking lot at the County Office Building. Explosives had been placed under a truck belonging to Sheriff Bud Oswald. Twenty-one injured by flying glass and debris, nine critically injured, eight with moderate injuries, including Sheriff Oswald, and four with minor injuries.
9:58 AM	Fire reported at 914 East Tenth, the home of Mr. and Mrs. Thornton. Detective Ned Shoemaker was the first on the scene. He was reporting the extent of the fire when he heard gunshots inside and a person ran from the building with hair and clothing on fire. Shoemaker used his coat to extinguish the flames and discovered that the victim, male,

had been shot twice, once each in the neck and chest. Based on a driver's license and other personal effects found on his body, the gunshot victim, pronounced dead at the scene, was determined to be Mr. Donovan.

10:08 AM Firefighters responded to the scene and began to suppress the fire.

1:22 PM Fire determined to be under control.

1:30 PM Investigators find the remains of a victim on the first floor just inside the front door. Phone calls to the high school determined that Mrs. Thornton had called in sick. She was later identified by her husband through her personal effects. He is currently in seclusion under a physician's care.

Detective Shoemaker received second- and third-degree burns on his hands and arms. He remains in a hospital in an undisclosed location for treatment of his injuries and has been placed on administrative leave pending his recovery.

Mr. Donovan has had a long history of violent behavior. He has been described by locals as a bully and is a suspect in at least two local arsons. He served two years in the Missouri State Penitentiary in Jefferson City for assaulting Larry Gilmore, cousin to Lucius Gilmore, shot to death yesterday. It is suspected that Donovan surprised Mrs. Thornton as he was setting fire to her home and that she shot him in self-defense. Funeral services and burial arrangements are not yet complete. Mrs. Thornton was a longtime member of the First Presbyterian Church of Raleigh. Mr. Gilmore attended the Southside AME Church. Mr. Donovan was not known to have any religious affiliation.

Members of the investigative task force noted difficulty in coordinating the responses of all the agencies involved in yesterday's events because of the use of multiple frequencies and call centers. They said it demonstrates the need for a centralized emergency reporting and response system to serve police, sheriff, hospital, ambulance, and fire districts alike.

Epilogue

▼

Millie's Honor

Tuesday, September 16, 1986

"If I do this right, no one will ever know," Raymond mumbled as he twisted around in his Chevy pickup to back out of the narrow garage. It was more difficult than he expected. Because he had to work in the darkness to avoid attracting attention, it took him until 2:46 AM to get everything loaded. Backing down the narrow driveway in the moonlight, he was careful to keep his wheels on the concrete tracks. He slowed when he got to the gutter where the rear bumper always dragged and eased out into the street, making as little noise as possible.

Jake's pickup stood in the moonlight at the opposite curb. He cranked the wheel sharply to the left to miss it. Pulling the gearshift lever down two thumps, he let the truck idle through the black tunnel of trees for a block and a half before he switched on his lights.

Just as he had every day for most of his life, he made a right turn onto Walnut at the Baptist Church. He drove past Wickell's Funeral Home on the left and the Raleigh Savings Bank on the right. The old brick pavement around the county courthouse made his tires rumble as he worked his way toward Highway 19. As far as he could tell, not a soul in Raleigh knew that he was back in business.

It was Millie's fault. Really, it was. He thought she'd gone mad that day in the Piggly Wiggly. It was embarrassing. All he wanted to do was to pay for three bags of groceries and get out of there. But he knew as soon as Millie started looking for Wally, the new store manager, that it wasn't going to happen. His beloved Millie, with those sparkling green eyes, had Walter Grayson backed up against the meat counter in nothing flat.

Raymond knew the signals. When Millie snatched her glasses off her face and stuck them in her wavy red hair, Walter was in trouble. For that matter, since she had been teaching at Raleigh High for nearly twenty years, every kid and most of the adults in town knew that signal. It meant look out. Miss Millie was setting things straight.

"Wally Grayson, I happen to know that you know better, because I taught you myself," Miss Millie said. "I don't care whether this store is part of a big chain or not. You know better than to let anyone put up a sign that says 'twenty items or less' at your checkout counter." She was shaking her finger at him now. "You know darn well that sign should read 'twenty items or fewer,' and don't you dare tell me you can't do anything about it! Since you're the manager of this grocery store, you need to fix that. Now don't let me come back in here and find that sign like that next time."

"Yes, Miss Millie. I'll get right on that, Miss Millie. Let me help you with those bags, Miss Millie."

They were quite a sight, the three of them marching out to the Chevy, Miss Millie with her nose still turned skyward in feigned indignation, Raymond embarrassed for his friend, and Wally, red-faced and speechless. If he hadn't rolled his eyes at Raymond the way he did in choir, they might've made it to the car. But three paces short, Raymond began to snicker. That was all Wally needed. Two basses fell into another one of their giggling fits. The fact that Millie was not pleased made it all the funnier.

"Boys, what on earth is the matter with you? You behave yourselves, now. C'mon, Raymond, let's get home before the ice cream melts."

Wally changed the signs with a marking pen when he got back in the store. Months later, after a spirited volley of letters to the editor, several of the stores around the area began installing new signs that read "twenty items or fewer."

On the day of Millie's funeral, every business in town shut down. They held the memorial service in the high school gymnasium. It was the only place in town that could accommodate all her students. It seemed natural somehow to have the pallbearers roll her casket across the basketball court. After all, she had never missed a game.

Less than six months after her passing, a billboard went up on Highway 19 that read, "Think your pregnant?" Two mornings later, the good people of Raleigh awoke to find the sign had been corrected in great slashing lines of bright orange paint to "Think you're pregnant?" But it was the big letter grade F and the message at the bottom that everyone in town recognized: "Grammar matters! It proves you're educated."

Over the next year, seven more billboards in Raleigh County received failing grades. One exception was the "Westminister Presbyterian Church" sign over by Claremont. It got a D+. It should have been "Westminster," but it was allowed to pass because it was a church sign. After all, that should count for something.

Wilkerson Outdoor Advertising wrote letters to Bud Oswald, the Raleigh County sheriff, complaining about having their signs vandalized. But they gave that up after one of their letters got published, misspellings and all, in the *Raleigh Journal-Messenger*. Sheriff Oswald's reply ran alongside it.

> Gentlemen, we share your concern about the recent crime wave involving the billboards in Raleigh County. Fortunately for us, a grammarian resides somewhere in these hills who has had the decency to do something about it. It is my fervent hope that one day we will be able to bring the guilty parties to justice. Until then, I respectfully submit that meticulous proofreading may be our only defense.

Raymond turned east onto Highway 19, taking note of the odometer. Exactly 3.7 miles later, he topped the ridge to see the sign that Sheriff Bud had told him about last Monday outside Dutch's Diner. The lunch crowd had gotten very quiet when Sheriff Oswald slid into the booth opposite him.

"Good afternoon, Raymond."

"Afternoon, Sheriff."

The chatter resumed after it became clear that Bud was only talking about the St. Louis Cardinals and last year's Fourth of July fireworks. Oswald certainly knew his town. Raymond and the sheriff ate and chatted about nothing in particular, paid their bills, and strolled amiably out toward Raymond's pickup together.

There, in the street, with his back to the faces staring out at them from the restaurant window, Sheriff Oswald took care of business.

"You know, Raymond, this sign-grading business reminds me of Miss Millie. Can't tell you how many times she wrote, 'Grammar counts!' on my papers. I'd sure like to know what she thinks of this. It's a shame she's not here to tell us. But there's this sign out on Highway 19, about four miles east of here, that would make her have a cow."

"No fooling? What's it say?"

"Bold as daylight, it says, 'Are you paying to much interest?' Spelled 't-o' instead of 't-o-o.'"

"Does it belong to Wilkerson Outdoor Advertising?"

"Yep. I'm afraid so. Raymond, it seems like this crime spree will never end."

"I don't know what to tell you, Bud, but I'm pretty sure you're right about how Millie would react. Wish there was something I could do, but I don't know any more about it than you do."

"Well, that's what I thought. It's been good talking to you, Raymond. You take care now, y'hear?"

"You too, Bud. See you."

On Wednesday morning, Raymond carried his coffee out onto the front porch and placed it on the top railing. He sat down on the steps and flipped open the paper. There, just as he'd expected, were the headlines on page one, above the fold. Millie would have been proud.

Midnight Grammarian Strikes Again

It was a magnificent morning. Raymond leaned back on his elbows and took in a deep breath of Raleigh morning air. It was good to be a free man in a town like this, where people mattered and the right things made a difference. The morning sunlight glinted brightly off the moisture pooling around his eyes and racing down his cheeks. He closed his eyes and thought of his beautiful Millicent.

The End

978-0-595-47224-6
0-595-47224-9